Clematis:
Mental Beauty

Struggling against the mysterious forces of her own mental "beauty," A.J. knew her survival depended upon keeping her feelings under control. Still, unfulfilled passions burned within her—and David Brady's unflagging attentions were merely adding fuel to the flames!

NORA ROBERTS

LANGUAGE OF LOVE

**Love has a language all its own, and for
centuries, flowers have symbolized
love's finest expression.
Discover the language of flowers
—and love—
in this romantic collection of 48 favorite
books by bestselling author Nora Roberts.**

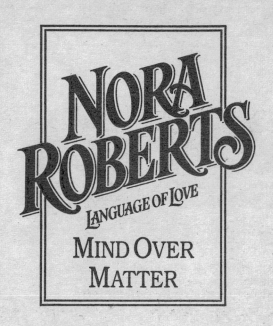

NORA ROBERTS

LANGUAGE OF LOVE

MIND OVER MATTER

Silhouette Books®

SILHOUETTE BOOKS
300 East 42nd St., New York, N.Y. 10017

MIND OVER MATTER © 1987 by Nora Roberts.
First published as a Silhouette Intimate Moments.

Language of Love edition published January 1992.

ISBN: 0-373-51045-4

Printed in U.S.A.

Chapter One

He'd expected a crystal ball, pentagrams and a few tea leaves. Burning candles and incense wouldn't have surprised him. Though he wouldn't admit it to anyone, he'd actually looked forward to it. As a producer of documentaries for public television, David Brady dealt in hard facts and meticulous research. Anything and everything that went into one of his productions was checked and rechecked, most often personally. The truth was, he'd thought an afternoon with a fortune teller would bring him a refreshing, even comic relief from the daily pressure of scripts, storyboards and budgets. She didn't even wear a turban.

The woman who opened the door of the comfortable suburban home in Newport Beach looked as though she would more likely be found at a bridge table than a séance. She smelled of lilacs and dusting powder, not musk and mystery. David's impression that she was housekeeper or companion to the renowned psychic was immediately disabused.

"Hello." She offered a small, attractive hand and a smile. "I'm Clarissa DeBasse. Please come in, Mr. Brady. You're right on time."

"Miss DeBasse." David adjusted his thinking and accepted her hand. He'd done enough research so far to be prepared for the normalcy of people involved in the paranormal. "I appreciate your seeing me. Should I wonder how you know who I am?"

As their hands linked, she let impressions of him come and go, to be sorted out later. Intuitively she felt he was a man she could trust and rely on. It was enough for the moment. "I could claim precognition, but I'm afraid it's simple logic. You were expected at one-thirty." Her agent had called to remind her, or Clarissa would still be knee-deep in her vegetable garden. "I suppose it's possible you're carrying brushes and samples in that briefcase, but I have the feeling it's papers and contracts. Now I'm sure you'd like some coffee after your drive down from L.A."

"Right again." He stepped into a cozy living room with pretty blue curtains and a wide couch that sagged noticeably in the middle.

"Sit down, Mr. Brady. I just brought the tray out, so the coffee's hot."

Deciding the couch was unreliable, David chose a chair and waited while Clarissa sat across from him and poured coffee into two mismatched cups and saucers. It took him only a moment to study and analyze. He was a man who leaned heavily on first impressions. She looked, as she offered cream and sugar, like anyone's favorite aunt—rounded without being really plump, neat without being stiff. Her face was soft and pretty and had lined little in fifty-odd years. Her pale blond hair was cut stylishly and showed no gray, which David attributed to her hairdresser. She was entitled to her vanity, he thought. When she offered the cup, he noted the symphony of rings on her hands. That, at least, was in keeping with the image he had projected.

"Thank you. Miss DeBasse, I have to tell you, you're not at all what I expected."

Comfortable with herself, she settled back. "You were expecting me to greet you at the door with a crystal ball in my hands and a raven on my shoulder."

The amusement in her eyes would have had some men shifting in their chairs. David only lifted a brow. "Something like that.'' He sipped his coffee. The fact that it was hot was the only thing going for it. ''I've read quite a bit about you in the past few weeks. I also saw a tape of your appearance on the *Barrow Show*.'' He probed gently for the right phrasing. ''You have a different image on camera.''

''That's show biz,'' she said so casually he wondered if she was being sarcastic. Her eyes remained clear and friendly. ''I don't generally discuss business, particularly at home, but since it seemed important that you see me, I thought we'd be more comfortable this way.'' She smiled again, showing the faintest of dimples in her cheeks. ''I've disappointed you.''

''No.'' And he meant it. ''No, you haven't.'' Because his manners went only so far, he put the coffee down. ''Miss DeBasse—''

''Clarissa.'' She beamed such a bright smile at him he had no trouble returning it.

''Clarissa, I want to be honest with you.''

''Oh, that's always best.'' Her voice was soft and sincere as she folded her hands on her lap.

''Yeah.'' The childlike trust in her eyes threw him for a moment. If she was a hard-edged, money-oriented con, she was doing a good job disguising it. ''I'm a very practical man. Psychic phenomena, clairvoyance, telepathy and that sort of thing, don't fit into my day-to-day life.''

She only smiled at him, understanding. Whatever thoughts came into her head remained there. This time David did shift in his chair.

''I decided to do this series on parapsychology mainly for its entertainment value.''

''You don't have to apologize.'' She lifted her hand just as a large black cat leaped into her lap. Without looking at it, Clarissa stroked it from head to tail. ''You see, David, someone in my position understands perfectly the doubts and the fascination people have for... such things. I'm not a radical." As the cat curled up in her lap, she continued to pet it, looking calm and content. "I'm simply a person who's been given a gift, and a certain responsibility."

"A responsibility?" He started to reach in his pocket for his cigarettes, then noticed there were no ashtrays.

"Oh, yes." As she spoke, Clarissa opened the drawer of the coffee table and took out a small blue dish. "You can use this," she said in passing, then settled back again. "A young boy might receive a toolbox for his birthday. It's a gift. He has choices to make. He can use his new tools to learn, to build, to repair. He can also use them to saw the legs off tables. He could also put the toolbox in his closet and forget about it. A great many of us do the last, because the tools are too complicated or simply too overwhelming. Have you ever had a psychic experience, David?"

He lit a cigarette. "No."

"No?" There weren't many people who would give such a definitive no. "Never a sense of déjà vu, perhaps?"

He paused a moment, interested. "I suppose everyone's had a sense of doing something before, being somewhere before. A feeling of mixed signals."

"Perhaps. Intuition, then."

"You consider intuition a psychic gift?"

"Oh, yes." Enthusiasm lit her face and made her eyes young. "Of course it depends entirely on how it's developed, how it's channeled, how it's used. Most of us use only a fraction of what we have because our minds are so crowded with other things."

"Was it impulse that led you to Matthew Van Camp?"

A shutter seemed to come down over her eyes. "No."

Again he found her puzzling. The Van Camp case was the one that had brought her prominently into the public eye. He would have thought she would have been anxious to speak of it, elaborate, yet she seemed to close down at the mention of the name. David blew out smoke and noticed that the cat was watching him with bored but steady eyes. "Clarissa, the Van Camp case is ten years old, but it's still one of the most celebrated and controversial of your successes."

"That's true. Matthew is twenty now. A very handsome young man."

"There are some who believe he'd be dead if Mrs. Van Camp hadn't fought both her husband and the police to have you brought in on the kidnapping."

"And there are some who believe the entire thing was staged for publicity," she said so calmly as she sipped from her cup. "Alice Van Camp's next movie was quite a box office success. Did you see the film? It was wonderful."

He wasn't a man to be eased offtrack when he'd already decided on a destination. "Clarissa, if you agree to be part of this documentary, I'd like you to talk about the Van Camp case."

She frowned a bit, pouted almost, as she petted her cat. "I don't know if I can help you there, David. It was a very traumatic experience for the Van Camps, very traumatic. Bringing it all up again could be painful for them."

He hadn't reached his level of success without knowing how and when to negotiate. "If the Van Camps agreed?"

"Oh, then that's entirely different." While she considered, the cat stirred in her lap, then began to purr loudly. "Yes, entirely different. You know, David, I admire your work. I saw your documentary on child abuse. It was gripping and very upsetting."

"It was meant to be."

"Yes, exactly." She could have told him a great deal of the world was upsetting, but didn't think he was ready to understand how she knew, and how she dealt with it. "What is it you're looking for with this?"

"A good show." When she smiled he was sure he'd been right not to try to con her. "One that'll make people think and question."

"Will you?"

He tapped out his cigarette. "I produce. How much I question I suppose depends on you."

It seemed like not only the proper answer, but the truest one. "I like you, David. I think I'd like to help you."

"I'm glad to hear that. You'll want to look over the contract and—"

"No," she cut him off as he reached for his briefcase. "Details." She explained them away with a gesture of her hand. "I let my agent bother with those things."

"Fine." He'd feel more comfortable discussing terms with an agent. "I'll send them over if you give me a name."

"The Fields Agency in Los Angeles."

She'd surprised him again. The comfortable auntlike lady had one of the most influential and prestigious agencies on the coast. "I'll have them sent over this afternoon. I'd enjoy working with you, Clarissa."

"May I see your palm?"

Every time he thought he had her catalogued, she shifted on him. Still, humoring her was easy. David offered his hand. "Am I going to take an ocean voyage?"

She was neither amused nor offended. Though she took his hand, palm up, she barely glanced at it. Instead she studied him with eyes that seemed abruptly cool. She saw a man in his early thirties, attractive in a dark, almost brooding way despite the well-styled black hair and casually elegant clothes. The bones in his face were strong, angular enough to warrant a second glance. His brows were thick, as black as his hair, and dominated surprisingly quiet eyes. Or their cool, pale green appeared quiet at first glance. She saw a mouth that was firm, full enough to gain a woman's attention. The hand in hers was wide, long fingered, artistic. It vied with a rangy, athletic build. But she saw beyond that.

"You're a very strong man, physically, emotionally, intellectually."

"Thank you."

"Oh, I don't flatter, David." It was a gentle, almost maternal reproof. "You haven't yet learned how to temper this strength with tenderness in your relationships. I suppose that's why you've never married."

She had his attention now, reluctantly. But he wasn't wearing a ring, he reminded himself. And anyone who cared to find out about his marital status had only to make a few inquiries. "The standard response is I've never met the right woman."

"In this case it's perfectly true. You need to find someone every bit as strong as you are. You will, sooner than you think. It won't be easy, of course, and it will only work between you if you both remember the tenderness I just spoke of."

"So I'm going to meet the right woman, marry and live happily ever after?"

"I don't tell the future, ever." Her expression changed again, becoming placid. "And I only read palms of people who interest me. Shall I tell you what my intuition tells me, David?"

"Please."

"That you and I are going to have an interesting and long-term relationship." She patted his hand before she released it. "I'm going to enjoy that."

"So am I." He rose. "I'll see you again, Clarissa."

"Yes. Yes, of course." She rose and nudged the cat onto the floor. "Run along now, Mordred."

"Mordred?" David repeated as the cat jumped up to settle himself on the sagging sofa cushion.

"Such a sad figure in folklore," Clarissa explained. "I always felt he got a bad deal. After all, we can't escape our destiny, can we?"

For the second time David felt her cool, oddly intimate gaze on him. "I suppose not," he murmured, and let her lead him to the door.

"I've so enjoyed our chat, David. Please come back again."

David stepped out into the warm spring air and wondered why he felt certain he would.

"Of course he's an excellent producer, Abe. I'm just not sure he's right for Clarissa."

A. J. Fields paced around her office in the long, fluid gait that always masked an overflow of nervous energy. She stopped to straighten a picture that was slightly tilted before she turned back to her associate. Abe Ebbitt was sitting with his hands folded on his round belly, as was his habit. He didn't bother to push back the glasses that had fallen down his nose. He watched A.J. patiently before he reached up to scratch one of the two clumps of hair on either side of his head.

"A.J., the offer is very generous."

"She doesn't need the money."

His agent's blood shivered at the phrase, but he continued to speak calmly. "The exposure."

"Is it the right kind of exposure?"

"You're too protective of Clarissa, A.J."

"That's what I'm here for," she countered. Abruptly she stopped, and sat on the corner of her desk. When Abe saw her brows draw together, he fell silent. He might speak to her when she was in this mood, but she wouldn't answer. He respected and admired her. Those were the reasons he, a veteran Hollywood agent, was working for the Fields Agency, instead of carving up the town on his own. He was old enough to be her father, and realized that a decade before their roles would have been reversed. The fact that he worked for her didn't bother him in the least. The best, he was fond of saying, never minded answering to the best. A minute passed, then two.

"She's made up her mind to do it," A.J. muttered, but again Abe remained silent. "I just—" Have a feeling, she thought. She hated to use that phrase. "I just hope it isn't a mistake. The wrong director, the wrong format, and she could be made to look like a fool. I won't have that, Abe."

"You're not giving Clarissa enough credit. You know better than to let your emotions color a business deal, A.J."

"Yeah, I know better." That's why she was the best. A.J. folded her arms and reminded herself of it. She'd learned at a very young age how to channel emotion. It had been more than necessary; it had been vital. When you grew up in a house where your widowed mother often forgot little details like the mortgage payment, you learned how to deal with business in a businesslike way or you went under. She was an agent because she enjoyed the wheeling and dealing. And because she was damn good at it. Her Century City office with its lofty view of Los Angeles was proof of just how good. Still, she hadn't gotten there by making deals blindly.

"I'll decide after I meet with Brady this afternoon."

Abe grinned at her, recognizing the look. "How much more are you going to ask for?"

"I think another ten percent." She picked up a pencil and tapped it against her palm. "But first I intend to find out exactly what's going into this documentary and what angles he's going for."

"Word is Brady's tough."

She sent him a deceptively sweet smile that had fire around the edges. "Word is so am I."

"He hasn't got a prayer." He rose, tugging at his belt. "I've got a meeting. Let me know how it goes."

"Sure." She was already frowning at the wall when he closed the door.

David Brady. The fact that she personally admired his work would naturally influence her decision. Still, at the right time and for the right fee, she would sign a client to play a tea bag in a thirty-second local commercial. Clarissa was a different matter. Clarissa DeBasse had been her first client. Her only client, A.J. remembered, during those first lean years. If she was protective of her, as Abe had said, A.J. felt she had a right to be. David Brady might be a successful producer of quality documentaries for public television, but he had to prove himself to A. J. Fields before Clarissa signed on the dotted line.

There'd been a time when A.J. had had to prove herself. She hadn't started out with a staff of fifteen in an exclusive suite of offices. Ten years before, she'd been scrambling for clients and hustling deals from an office that had consisted of a phone booth outside a corner deli. She'd lied about her age. Not too many people had been willing to trust their careers to an eighteen-year-old. Clarissa had.

A.J. gave a little sigh as she worked out a kink in her shoulder. Clarissa didn't really consider what she did, or what she had, a career as much as a calling. It was up to A.J. to haggle over the details.

She was used to it. Her mother had always been such a warm, generous woman. But details had never been her strong point. As a child, it had been up to A.J. to remember when the bills were due. She'd balanced the checkbook, discouraged door-to-door salesmen and juggled her schoolwork with the household budget. Not that her mother was a fool, or neglectful of her daughter. There had always been love, conversation and interest. But their roles had so often been reversed. It was the mother who would claim the stray puppy had followed her home and the daughter who had worried how to feed it.

Still, if her mother had been different, wouldn't A.J. herself be different? That was a question that surfaced often. Destiny was something that couldn't be outmaneuvered. With a laugh, A.J. rose. Clarissa would love that one, she mused.

Walking around her desk, she let herself sink into the deep, wide-armed chair her mother had given her. The chair, unlike the heavy, clean-lined desk, was extravagant and impractical. Who else would have had a chair made in cornflower-blue leather because it matched her daughter's eyes?

A.J. realigned her thoughts and picked up the DeBasse contract. It was in the center of a desk that was meticulously in order. There were no photographs, no flowers, no cute paperweights. Everything on or in her desk had a purpose, and the purpose was business.

She had time to give the contract one more thorough going-over before her appointment with David Brady. Before she met with him, she would understand every phrase, every clause and every alternative. She was just making a note on the final clause, when her buzzer rang. Still writing, A.J. cradled the phone at her ear.

"Yes, Diane."

"Mr. Brady's here, A.J."

"Okay. Any fresh coffee?"

"We have sludge at the moment. I can make some."

"Only if I buzz you. Bring him back, Diane."

She turned her notepad back to the first page, then rose as the door opened. "Mr. Brady." A.J. extended her hand, but stayed behind her desk. It was, she'd learned, important to establish certain positions of power right from the start. Besides, the time it took him to cross the office gave her an opportunity to study and judge. He looked more like someone she might have for a client than a producer. Yes, she was certain she could have sold that hard, masculine look and rangy walk. The laconic, hard-boiled detective on a weekly series; the solitary, nomadic cowboy in a feature film. Pity.

David had his own chance for study. He hadn't expected her to be so young. She was attractive in that streamlined, no-nonsense sort of way he could respect professionally and ignore personally. Her body seemed almost too slim in the sharply tailored suit that was rescued from dullness by a fire-engine-red blouse. Her pale blond hair was cut in a deceptively casual style that shagged around the ears, then angled back to sweep her collar. It suited the honey-toned skin that had been kissed by the sun—or a sunlamp. Her face was oval, her mouth just short of being too wide. Her eyes were a rich blue, accentuated by clever smudges of shadow and framed now with oversize glasses. Their hands met, held and released as hands in business do dozens of times every day.

"Please sit down, Mr. Brady. Would you like some coffee?"

"No, thank you." He took a chair and waited until she settled behind the desk. He noticed that she folded her hands over the contract. No rings, no bracelets, he mused. Just a slender, black-banded watch. "It seems we have a number of mutual acquaintances, Ms. Fields. Odd that we haven't met before."

"Yes, isn't it?" She gave him a small, noncommittal smile. "But, then, as an agent, I prefer staying in the background. You met Clarissa DeBasse."

"Yes, I did." So they'd play stroll around the bush for a while, he decided, and settled back. "She's charming. I have to admit, I'd expected someone, let's say, more eccentric."

This time A.J.'s smile was both spontaneous and generous. If David had been thinking about her on a personal level, his opinion would have changed. "Clarissa is never quite what one expects. Your project sounds interesting, Mr.

Brady, but the details I have are sketchy. I'd like you to tell me just what it is you plan to produce."

"A documentary on psychic phenomena, or Psi, as I'm told it's called in studies, touching on clairvoyance, parapsychology, ESP, palmistry, telepathy and spiritualism."

"Séances and haunted houses, Mr. Brady?"

He caught the faint disapproval in her tone and wondered about it. "For someone with a psychic for a client, you sound remarkably cynical."

"My client doesn't talk to departed souls or read tea leaves." A.J. sat back in the chair in a way she knew registered confidence and position. "Miss DeBasse has proved herself many times over to be an extraordinarily sensitive woman. She's never claimed to have supernatural powers."

"Supernormal."

She drew in a quiet breath. "You've done your homework. Yes, 'supernormal' is the correct term. Clarissa doesn't believe in overstatements."

"Which is one of the reasons I want Clarissa DeBasse for my program."

A.J. noted the easy use of the possessive pronoun. Not the program, but *my* program. David Brady obviously took his work personally. So much the better, she decided. Then he wouldn't care to look like a fool. "Go on."

"I've talked to mediums, palmists, entertainers, scientists, parapsychologists and carnival gypsies. You'd be amazed at the range of personalities."

A.J. stuck her tongue in her cheek. "I'm sure I would."

Though he noticed her amusement, he let it pass. "They run from the obviously fake to the absolutely sincere. I've spoken with heads of parapsychology departments in several well-known institutions. Every one of them mentioned Clarissa's name."

"Clarissa's been generous with herself." Again he thought he detected slight disapproval. "Particularly in the areas of research and testing."

And there would be no ten percent there. He decided that explained her attitude. "I intend to show possibilities, ask questions. The audience will come up with its own answers. In the five one-hour segments I have, I'll have room to touch on everything from cold spots to tarot cards."

In a gesture she thought she'd conquered long ago, she drummed her fingers on the desk. "And where does Miss DeBasse fit in?"

She was his ace in the hole. But he wasn't ready to play her yet. "Clarissa is a recognizable name. A woman who's 'proved herself,' to use your phrase, to be extraordinarily sensitive. Then there's the Van Camp case."

Frowning, A.J. picked up a pencil and began to run it through her fingers. "That was ten years ago."

"The child of a Hollywood star is kidnapped, snatched from his devoted nanny as he plays in the park. The ransom call demands a half a million. The mother's frantic— the police are baffled. Thirty-six hours pass without a clue as the boy's parents desperately try to get the cash together. Over the father's objection, the mother calls a friend, a woman who did her astrological chart and occasionally reads palms. The woman comes, of course, and sits for an hour holding some of the boy's things—his baseball glove, a stuffed toy, the pajama top he'd worn to bed the night before. At the end of that hour, the woman gives the police a description of the boy's kidnappers and the exact location of the house where he's being held. She even describes the room where he's being held, down to the chipped paint on the ceiling. The boy sleeps in his own bed that night."

David pulled out a cigarette, lit it and blew out smoke, while A.J. remained silent. "Ten years doesn't take away that kind of impact, Ms. Fields. The audience will be just as fascinated today as they were then.''

It shouldn't have made her angry. It was sheer foolishness to respond that way. A.J. continued to sit silently as she worked back the surge of temper. ''A great many people call the Van Camp case a fraud. Dredging that up after ten years will only dredge up more criticism.''

''A woman in Clarissa's position must have to deal with criticism continually.'' He saw the flare come into her eyes— fierce and fast.

''That may be, but I have no intention of allowing her to sign a contract that guarantees it. I have no intention of seeing my client on a televised trial.''

''Hold it.'' He had a temper of his own and could respect hers—if he understood it. ''Clarissa goes on trial every time she's in the public eye. If her abilities can't stand up to cameras and questions, she shouldn't be doing what she does. As her agent, I'd think you'd have a stronger belief in her competence.''

''My beliefs aren't your concern.'' Intending to toss him and his contract out, A.J. started to rise, when the phone interrupted her. With an indistinguishable oath, she lifted the receiver. ''No calls, Diane. No—oh.'' A.J. set her teeth and composed herself. ''Yes, put her on.''

''Oh, I'm so sorry to bother you at work, dear.''

''That's all right. I'm in a meeting, so—''

''Oh, yes, I know.'' Clarissa's calm, apologetic voice came quietly in her ear. ''With that nice David Brady.''

''That's a matter of opinion.''

''I had a feeling you wouldn't hit it off the first time.'' Clarissa sighed and stroked her cat. ''I've been giving that contract business a great deal of thought.'' She didn't mention the dream, knowing her agent wouldn't want to hear it. ''I've decided I want to sign it right away. Now, now, I know what you're going to say,'' she continued before A.J. could say a word. "You're the agent—you handle the business. You do whatever you think best about clauses and such, but I want to do this program."

A.J. recognized the tone. Clarissa had a feeling. There was never any arguing with Clarissa's feelings. "We need to talk about this."

"Of course, dear, all you like. You and David iron out the details. You're so good at that. I'll leave all the terms up to you, but I will sign the contract."

With David sitting across from her, A.J. couldn't take the satisfaction of accepting defeat by kicking her desk. "All right. But I think you should know I have feelings of my own."

"Of course you do. Come to dinner tonight."

She nearly smiled. Clarissa loved to feed you to smooth things over. Pity she was such a dreadful cook. "I can't. I have a dinner appointment."

"Tomorrow."

"All right. I'll see you then."

After hanging up, A.J. took a deep breath and faced David again. "I'm sorry for the interruption."

"No problem."

"As there's nothing specific in the contract regarding the Van Camp case, including that in the program would be strictly up to Miss DeBasse."

"Of course. I've already spoken to her about it."

A.J. very calmly, very deliberately bit her tongue. "I see. There's also nothing specific about Miss DeBasse's position in the documentary. That will have to be altered."

"I'm sure we can work that out." So she was going to sign, David mused, and listened to a few other minor changes A.J. requested. Before the phone rang, she'd been ready to pitch him out. He'd seen it in her eyes. He held back a smile as they negotiated another minor point. He was no clairvoyant, but he would bet his grant that Clarissa

DeBasse had been on the other end of that phone. A. J. Fields had been caught right in the middle. Best place for agents, he thought, and settled back.

"We'll redraft the contract and have it to you tomorrow."

Everybody's in a hurry, she thought, and settled back herself. "Then I'm sure we can do business, Mr. Brady, if we can settle one more point."

"Which is?"

"Miss DeBasse's fee." A.J. flipped back the contract and adjusted the oversize glasses she wore for reading. "I'm afraid this is much less than Miss DeBasse is accustomed to accepting. We'll need another twenty percent."

David lifted a brow. He'd been expecting something along these lines, but he'd expected it sooner. Obviously A. J. Fields wasn't one of the top in her profession by doing the expected. "You understand we're working in public television. Our budget can't compete with network. As producer, I can offer another five percent, but twenty is out of reach."

"And five is inadequate." A.J. slipped off her glasses and dangled them by an earpiece. Her eyes seemed larger, richer, without them. "I understand public television, Mr. Brady, and I understand your grant." She gave him a charming smile. "Fifteen percent."

Typical agent, he thought, not so much annoyed as fatalistic. She wanted ten, and ten was precisely what his budget would allow. Still, there was a game to be played. "Miss DeBasse is already being paid more than anyone else on contract."

"You're willing to do that because she'll be your biggest draw. I also understand ratings."

"Seven."

"Twelve."

"Ten."

"Done." A.J. rose. Normally the deal would have left her fully satisfied. Because her temper wasn't completely under control it was difficult to appreciate the fact that she'd gotten exactly what she'd intended to get. "I'll look for the revised contracts."

"I'll send them by messenger tomorrow afternoon. That phone call..." He paused as he rose. "You wouldn't be dealing with me without it, would you?"

She studied him a moment and cursed him for being sharp, intelligent and intuitive. All the things she needed for her client. "No, I wouldn't."

"Be sure to thank Clarissa for me." With a smile smug enough to bring her temper back to boil he offered his hand.

"Goodbye, Mr...." When their hands met this time, her voice died. Feelings ran into her with the impact of a slap, leaving her weak and breathless. Apprehension, desire, fury and delight rolled through her at the touch of flesh to flesh. She had only a moment to berate herself for allowing temper to open the door.

"Ms. Fields?" She was staring at him, through him, as though he were an apparition just risen from the floorboards. In his, her hand was limp and icy. Automatically David took her arm. If he'd ever seen a woman about to faint, he was seeing one now. "You'd better sit down."

"What?" Though shaken, A.J. willed herself back. "No, no, I'm fine. I'm sorry, I must have been thinking of something else." But as she spoke, she broke all contact with him and stepped back. "Too much coffee, too little sleep." And stay away from me, she said desperately to herself as she leaned back on the desk. Just stay away. "I'm glad we could do business, Mr. Brady. I'll pass everything along to my client."

Her color was back, her eyes clear. Still David hesitated. A moment before she'd looked fragile enough to crumble in his hands. "Sit down."

"I beg your—"

"Damn it, sit." He took her by the elbow and nudged her into a chair. "Your hands are shaking." Before she could do anything about it, he was kneeling in front of her. "I'd advise canceling that dinner appointment and getting a good night's sleep."

She curled her hands together on her lap to keep him from touching her again. "There's no reason for you to be concerned."

"I generally take a personal interest when a woman all but faints at my feet."

The sarcastic tone settled the flutters in her stomach. "Oh, I'm sure you do." But then he took her face in his hand and had her jerking. "Stop that."

Her skin was as soft as it looked, but he would keep that thought for later. "Purely a clinical touch, Ms. Fields. You're not my type."

Her eyes chilled. "Where do I give thanks?"

He wondered why the cool outrage in her eyes made him want to laugh. To laugh, and to taste her. "Very good," he murmured, and straightened. "Lay off the coffee," he advised, and left her alone before he did something ridiculous.

And alone, A.J. brought her knees up to her chest and pressed her face to them. What was she going to do now? she demanded as she tried to squeeze herself into a ball. What in God's name was she going to do?

Chapter Two

A.J. seriously considered stopping for a hamburger before going on to dinner at Clarissa's. She didn't have the heart for it. Besides, if she was hungry enough she would be able to make a decent showing out of actually eating whatever Clarissa prepared.

With the sunroof open, she sat back and tried to enjoy the forty-minute drive from her office to the suburbs. Beside her was a slim leather portfolio that held the contracts David Brady's office had delivered, as promised. Since the changes she'd requested had been made, she couldn't grumble. There was absolutely no substantial reason for her to object to the deal, or to her client working with Brady. All she had was a feeling. She'd been working on that since the previous afternoon.

It had been overwork, she told herself. She hadn't felt anything but a quick, momentary dizziness because she'd stood so fast. She hadn't felt anything for or about David Brady.

But she had.

A.J. cursed herself for the next ten miles before she brought herself under control.

She couldn't afford to be the least bit upset when she arrived in Newport Beach. There was no hiding such things from a woman like Clarissa DeBasse. She would have to be able to discuss not only the contract terms, but David Brady himself with complete objectivity or Clarissa would home in like radar.

For the next ten miles she considered stopping at a phone booth and begging off. She didn't have the heart for that, either.

Relax, A.J. ordered herself, and tried to imagine she was home in her apartment, doing long, soothing yoga exercises. It helped, and as the tension in her muscles eased, she turned up the radio. She kept it high until she turned the engine off in front of the tidy suburban home she'd helped pick out.

A.J. always felt a sense of self-satisfaction as she strolled up the walk. The house suited Clarissa, with its neat green lawn and pretty white shutters. It was true that with the success of her books and public appearances Clarissa could afford a house twice as big in Beverly Hills. But nothing would fit her as comfortably as this tidy brick ranch.

Shifting the brown bag that held wine under her arm, A.J. pushed open the door she knew was rarely locked. "Hello! I'm a six foot two, three hundred and twenty pound burglar come to steal all your jewelry. Care to give me a hand?"

"Oh, did I forget to lock it again?" Clarissa came bustling out of the kitchen, wiping her hands on an already smeared and splattered apron. Her cheeks were flushed from the heat of the stove, her lips already curved in greeting.

"Yes, you forgot to lock it again." Even with an armload of wine, A.J. managed to hug her. Then she kissed both cheeks as she tried to unobtrusively sniff out what was going on in the kitchen.

"It's meat loaf," Clarissa told her. "I got a new recipe."

"Oh." A.J. might have managed the smile if she hadn't remembered the last meat loaf so clearly. Instead she concentrated on the woman. "You look wonderful. I'd swear you were running into L.A. and sneaking into Elizabeth Arden's once a week."

"Oh, I can't be bothered with all that. It's too much worrying that causes lines and sags, anyway. You should remember that."

"So I look like a hag, do I?" A.J. dropped her portfolio on the table and stepped out of her shoes.

"You know I didn't mean that, but I can tell you're worried about something."

"Dinner," A.J. told her, evading. "I only had time for a half a sandwich at lunch."

"There, I've told you a dozen times you don't eat properly. Come into the kitchen. I'm sure everything's about ready."

Satisfied that she'd distracted Clarissa, A.J. started to follow.

"Then you can tell me what's really bothering you."

"Doesn't miss a trick," A.J. muttered as the doorbell rang.

"Get that for me, will you?" Clarissa cast an anxious glance at the kitchen. "I really should check the brussels sprouts."

"Brussels sprouts?" A.J. could only grimace as Clarissa disappeared into the kitchen. "Bad enough I have to eat the meat loaf, but brussels sprouts. I should have had the hamburger." When she opened the door her brows were already lowered.

"You look thrilled to see me."

One hand still on the knob, she stared at David. "What are you doing here?"

"Having dinner." Without waiting for an invitation, David stepped forward and stood with her in the open doorway. "You're tall. Even without your shoes."

A.J. closed the door with a quiet snap. "Clarissa didn't explain this was a business dinner."

"I think she considers it purely social." He hadn't yet figured out why he hadn't gotten the very professional Ms.

Fields out of his mind. Maybe he'd get some answers before the evening was up. "Why don't we think of it that way—A.J.?"

Manners had been ingrained in her by a quietly determined mother. Trapped, A.J. nodded. "All right, David. I hope you enjoy living dangerously."

"I beg your pardon?"

She couldn't resist the smile. "We're having meat loaf." She took the bottle of champagne he held and examined the label. "This should help. Did you happen to have a big lunch?"

There was a light in her eyes he'd never noticed before. It was a laugh, a joke, and very appealing. "What are you getting at?"

She patted his shoulder. "Sometimes it's best to go into these things unprepared. Sit down and I'll fix you a drink."

"Aurora."

"Yes?" A.J. answered automatically before she bit her tongue.

"Aurora?" David repeated, experimenting with the way it sounded in his voice. "That's what the *A* stands for?"

When A.J. turned to him her eyes were narrowed. "If just one person in the business calls me that, I'll know exactly where they got it from. You'll pay."

He ran a finger down the side of his nose, but didn't quite hide the smile. "I never heard a thing."

"Aurora, was that—" Clarissa stopped in the kitchen doorway and beamed. "Yes, it was David. How lovely." She studied both of them, standing shoulder to shoulder just inside her front door. For the instant she concentrated, the aura around them was very clear and very bright. "Yes, how lovely," she repeated. "I'm so glad you came."

"I appreciate your asking me." Finding Clarissa as charming as he had the first time, David crossed to her. He took her hand, but this time brought it to his lips. Pleasure flushed her cheeks.

"Champagne, how nice. We'll open it after I sign the contracts." She glanced over his shoulder to see A.J. frowning. "Why don't you fix yourself and David a drink, dear? I won't be much longer."

A.J. thought of the contracts in her portfolio, and of her own doubts. Then she gave in. Clarissa would do precisely what Clarissa wanted to do. In order to protect her, she had to stop fighting it and accept. "I can guarantee the vodka— I bought it myself."

"Fine—on the rocks." David waited while she went to a cabinet and took out a decanter and glasses.

"She remembered the ice," A.J. said, surprised when she opened the brass bucket and found it full.

"You seem to know Clarissa very well."

"I do." A.J. poured two glasses, then turned. "She's much more than simply a client to me, David. That's why I'm concerned about this program."

He walked to her to take the glass. Strange, he thought, you only noticed her scent when you stood close, very close. He wondered if she used such a light touch to draw men to her or to block their way. "Why the concern?"

If they were going to deal with each other, honesty might help. A.J. glanced toward the kitchen and kept her voice low. "Clarissa has a tendency to be very open with certain people. Too open. She can expose too much of herself, and leave herself vulnerable to all manner of complications."

"Are you protecting her from me?"

A.J. sipped from her drink. "I'm trying to decide if I should."

"I like her." He reached out to twine a lock of A.J.'s hair around his finger, before either of them realized his intention. He dropped his hand again so quickly she didn't have the chance to demand it. "She's a very likable woman,"

David continued as he turned to wander around the room. He wasn't a man to touch a business associate, especially one he barely knew, in so casual a manner. To give himself distance, he walked to the window to watch birds flutter around a feeder in the side yard. The cat was out there, he noticed, sublimely disinterested as it sunned itself in a last patch of sunlight.

A.J. waited until she was certain her voice would be properly calm and professional. "I appreciate that, but your project comes first, I imagine. You want a good show, and you'll do whatever it takes to produce one."

"That's right." The problem was, he decided, that she wasn't as tailored and streamlined as she'd been the day before. Her blouse was soft and silky, the color of poppies. If she'd had a jacket to match the snug white skirt, she'd left it in her car. She was shoeless and her hair had been tossed by the wind. He took another drink. She still wasn't his type. "But I don't believe I have a reputation for exploiting people in order to get it. I do my job, A.J., and expect the same from anyone who works with me."

"Fair enough." She finished the unwanted drink. "My job is to protect Clarissa in every way."

"I don't see that we have a problem."

"There now, everything's ready." Clarissa came out to see her guests not shoulder to shoulder, but with the entire room between them. Sensitive to mood, she felt the tension, confusion and distrust. Quite normal, she decided, for two stubborn, self-willed people on opposing ends. She wondered how long it would take them to admit attraction, let alone accept it. "I hope you're both hungry."

A.J. set down her empty glass with an easy smile. "David tells me he's starved. You'll have to give him an extra portion."

"Wonderful." Delighted, she led the way into the dining area. "I love to eat by candlelight, don't you?" She had a pair of candles burning on the table, and another half-dozen tapers on the sideboard. A.J. decided the romantic light definitely helped the looks of the meat loaf. "Aurora brought the wine, so I'm sure it's lovely. You pour, David, and I'll serve."

"It looks wonderful," he told her, and wondered why A.J. muffled a chuckle.

"Thank you. Are you from California originally, David?" Clarissa asked as she handed A.J. a platter.

"No, Washington State." He tipped Beaujolais into Clarissa's glass.

"Beautiful country." She handed Aurora a heaping bowl of mashed potatoes. "But so cold."

He could remember the long, windy winters with some nostalgia. "I didn't have any trouble acclimating to L.A."

"I grew up in the East and came out here with my husband nearly thirty years ago. In the fall I'm still the tiniest bit homesick for Vermont. You haven't taken any vegetables, Aurora. You know how I worry that you don't eat properly."

A.J. added brussels sprouts to her plate and hoped she'd be able to ignore them. "You should take a trip back this year," A.J. told Clarissa. One bite of the meat loaf was enough. She reached for the wine.

"I think about it. Do you have any family, David?"

He'd just had his first experience with Clarissa's cooking and hadn't recovered. He wondered what recipe she'd come across that called for leather. "Excuse me?"

"Any family?"

"Yes." He glanced at A.J. and saw the knowing smirk. "Two brothers and a sister scattered around Washington and Oregon."

"I came from a big family myself. I thoroughly enjoyed my childhood." Reaching out, she patted A.J.'s hand. "Aurora was an only child."

With a laugh A.J. gave Clarissa's hand a quick squeeze. "And I thoroughly enjoyed my childhood." Because she saw David politely making his way through a hill of lumpy potatoes, she felt a little tug on her conscience. A.J. waited until it passed. "What made you choose documentaries, David?"

"I'd always been fascinated by little films." Picking up the salt, he used it liberally. "With a documentary, the plot's already there, but it's up to you to come up with the angles, to find a way to present it to an audience and make them care while they're being entertained."

"Isn't it more of a learning experience?"

"I'm not a teacher." Bravely he dipped back into the meat loaf. "You can entertain with truth and speculation just as satisfyingly as you can entertain with fiction."

Somehow watching him struggle with the meal made it more palatable for her. "No urge to produce the big film?"

"I like television," he said easily, and reached for the wine. They were all going to need it. "I happen to think there's too much pap and not enough substance."

A.J.'s brow lifted, to disappear under a thin fringe of bangs. "Pap?"

"Unfortunately network television's rife with it. Shows like *Empire*, for instance, or *It Takes Two*."

"Really." A.J. leaned forward. "*Empire* has been a top-rated show for four years." She didn't add that it was a personal favorite.

"My point exactly. If a show like that retains consistently high ratings—a show that relies on steam, glitter and contrivance—it proves that the audience is being fed a steady stream of garbage."

"Not everyone feels a show has to be educational or 'good' for it to be quality. The problem with public television is that it has its nose up in the air so often the average American ignores it. After working eight hours, fighting traffic, coping with children and dealing with car repair bills, a person's entitled to relax.''

"Absolutely." Amazing, he thought, how lovely she became when you lit a little fire under her. Maybe she was a woman who needed conflict in her life. "But that same person doesn't have to shut off his or her intelligence to be entertained. That's called escapism."

"I'm afraid I don't watch enough television to see the difference," Clarissa commented, pleased to see her guests clearing their plates. "But don't you represent that lovely woman who plays on *Empire*?"

"Audrey Cummings." A.J. slipped her fingers under the cup of her wineglass and swirled it lightly. "A very accomplished actress, who's also played Shakespeare. We've just made a deal to have her take the role of Maggie in a remake of *Cat on a Hot Tin Roof*." The success of that deal was still sweet. Sipping her wine, she tilted her head at David. "For a play that deals in a lot of steam and sweat, it's amazing what longevity it's had. We can't claim it's a Verdi opera, can we?"

"There's more to public television than Verdi." He'd touched a nerve, he realized. But, then, so had she. "I don't suppose you caught the profile on Taylor Brooks? I thought it was one of the most detailed and informative on a rock star I'd ever seen." He picked up his wine in a half toast. "You don't represent him, too, do you?"

"No." She decided to play it to the hilt. "We dated casually a couple of years ago. I have a rule about keeping business and personal relationships separated."

"Wise." He lifted his wine and sipped. "Very wise."

"Unlike you, I have no prejudices when it comes to television. If I did, you'd hardly be signing one of my top clients."

"More meat loaf?" Clarissa asked.

"I couldn't eat another bite." A.J. smiled at David. "Perhaps David would like more."

"As much as I appreciate the home cooking, I can't." He tried not to register too much relief as he stood. "Let me help you clear up."

"Oh, no." Rising, Clarissa brushed his offer aside. "It relaxes me. Aurora, I think David was just a bit disappointed with me the first time we met. Why don't you show him my collection?"

"All right." Picking up her wineglass, A.J. gestured to him to follow. "You've scored points," she commented. "Clarissa doesn't show her collection to everyone."

"I'm flattered." But he took her by the elbow to stop her as they started down a narrow hallway. "You'd prefer it if I kept things strictly business with Clarissa."

A.J. lifted the glass to her lips and watched him over the rim. She'd prefer, for reasons she couldn't name, that he stayed fifty miles from Clarissa. And double that from her. "Clarissa chooses her own friends."

"And you make damn sure they don't take advantage of her."

"Exactly. This way." Turning, she walked to a door on the left and pushed it open. "It'd be more effective by candlelight, even more with a full moon, but we'll have to make do." A.J. flicked on the light and stepped out of his view.

It was an average-size room, suitable to a modern ranch house. Here, the windows were heavily draped to block the view of the yard—or to block the view inside. It wasn't difficult to see why Clarissa would use the veil to discourage the curious. The room belonged in a tower—or a dungeon.

Here was the crystal ball he'd expected. Unable to resist, David crossed to a tall, round-topped stand to examine it. The glass was smooth and perfect, reflecting only the faintest hint of the deep blue cloth beneath it. Tarot cards, obviously old and well used, were displayed in a locked case.

At a closer look he saw they'd been hand painted. A bookshelf held everything from voodoo to telekinesis. On the shelf with them was a candle in the shape of a tall, slender woman with arms lifted to the sky.

A Ouija board was set out on a table carved with pentagrams. One wall was lined with masks of pottery, ceramic, wood, even papier-mâché. There were dowsing rods and pendulums. A glass cabinet held pyramids of varying sizes. There was more—an Indian rattle, worn and fragile with age, Oriental worry beads in jet, others in amethyst.

"More what you expected?" A.J. asked after a moment.

"No." He picked up another crystal, this one small enough to rest in the palm of his hand. "I stopped expecting this after the first five minutes."

It was the right thing for him to say. A.J. sipped her wine again and tried not to be too pleased. "It's just a hobby with Clarissa, collecting the obvious trappings of the trade."

"She doesn't use them?"

"A hobby only. Actually, it started a long time ago. A friend found those tarot cards in a little shop in England and gave them to her. After that, things snowballed."

The crystal was cool and smooth in his hand as he studied her. "You don't approve?"

A.J. merely shrugged her shoulders. "I wouldn't if she took it seriously."

"Have you ever tried this?" He indicated the Ouija board.

"No."

It was a lie. He wasn't sure why she told it, or why he was certain of it. "So you don't believe in any of this."

"I believe in Clarissa. The rest of this is just showmanship."

Still, he was intrigued with it, intrigued with the fascination it held for people through the ages. "You've never been tempted to ask her to look in the crystal for you?"

"Clarissa doesn't need the crystal, and she doesn't tell the future."

He glanced into the clear glass in his hand. "Odd, you'd think if she can do the other things she's reported to be able to do, she could do that."

"I didn't say she couldn't—I said she doesn't."

David looked up from the crystal again. "Explain."

"Clarissa feels very strongly about destiny, and the tampering with it. She's refused, even for outrageous fees, to predict."

"But you're saying she could."

"I'm saying she chooses not to. Clarissa considers her gift a responsibility. Rather than misuse it in any way, she'd push it out of her life."

"Push it out." He set the crystal down. "Do you mean she—a psychic—could just refuse to be one. Just block out the... let's say power, for lack of a better term. Just turn it off?"

Her fingers had dampened on the glass. A.J. casually switched it to her other hand. "To a large extent, yes. You have to be open to it. You're a receptacle, a transmitter—the extent to which you receive or transmit depends on you."

"You seem to know a great deal about it."

He was sharp, she remembered abruptly. Very sharp. A.J. smiled deliberately and moved her shoulders again. "I know a great deal about Clarissa. If you spend any amount of time with her over the next couple of months, you'll know quite a bit yourself."

David walked to her. He watched her carefully as he took the wineglass from her and sipped himself. It was warm now and seemed more potent. "Why do I get the impression that you're uncomfortable in this room. Or is it that you're uncomfortable with me?"

"Your intuition's missing the mark. If you'd like, Clarissa can give you a few exercises to sharpen it."

"Your palms are damp." He took her hand, then ran his fingers down to the wrist. "Your pulse is fast. I don't need intuition to know that."

It was important—vital—that she keep calm. She met his eyes levelly and hoped she managed to look amused. "That probably has more to do with the meat loaf."

"The first time we met you had a very strong, very strange reaction to me."

She hadn't forgotten. It had given her a very restless night. "I explained—"

"I didn't buy it," he interrupted. "I still don't. That might be because I found myself doing a lot of thinking about you."

She'd taught herself to hold her ground. She'd had to. A.J. made one last attempt to do so now, though his eyes seemed much too quiet and intrusive, his voice too firm. She took her wineglass back from him and drained it. She learned it was a mistake, because she could taste him as well as the wine. "David, try to remember I'm not your type." Her voice was cool and faintly cutting. If she'd thought about it a few seconds longer, she would have realized it was the wrong tactic.

"No, you're not." His hand cupped her nape, then slid up into her hair. "But what the hell."

When he leaned closer, A.J. saw two clear-cut choices. She could struggle away and run for cover, or she could meet him with absolute indifference. Because the second choice seemed the stronger, she went with it. It was her next mistake.

He knew how to tempt a woman. How to coax. When his lips lowered to hers they barely touched, while his hand continued to stroke her neck and hair. A.J.'s grip on the wineglass tightened, but she didn't move, not forward, not away. His lips skimmed hers again, with just the hint of his tongue. The breath she'd been holding shuddered out.

As her eyes began to close, as her bones began to soften, he moved away from her mouth to trace his lips over her jaw. Neither of them noticed when the wineglass slipped out of her hand to land on the carpet.

He'd been right about how close you had to get to be tempted by her scent. It was strong and dark and private, as though it came through her pores to hover on her skin. As he brought his lips back to hers, he realized it wasn't something he'd forget. Nor was she.

This time her lips were parted, ready, willing. Still he moved slowly, more for his own sake now. This wasn't the cool man-crusher he'd expected, but a warm, soft woman who could draw you in with vulnerability alone. He needed time to adjust, time to think. When he backed away he still hadn't touched her, and had given her only the merest hint of a kiss. They were both shaken.

"Maybe the reaction wasn't so strange after all, Aurora," he murmured. "Not for either of us."

Her body was on fire; it was icy; it was weak. She couldn't allow her mind to follow suit. Drawing all her reserves of strength, A.J. straightened. "If we're going to be doing business—"

"And we are."

She let out a long, patient breath at the interruption. "Then you'd better understand the ground rules. I don't sleep around, not with clients, not with associates."

It pleased him. He wasn't willing to ask himself why. "Narrows the field, doesn't it?"

"That's my business," she shot back. "My personal life is entirely separate from my profession."

"Hard to do in this town, but admirable. However..." He couldn't resist reaching up to play with a stray strand of hair at her ear. "I didn't ask you to sleep with me."

She caught his hand by the wrist to push it away. It both surprised and pleased her to discover his pulse wasn't any steadier than hers. "Forewarned, you won't embarrass yourself by doing so and being rejected."

"Do you think I would?" He brought his hand back up to stroke a finger down her cheek. "Embarrass myself."

"Stop it."

He shook his head and studied her face again. Attractive, yes. Not beautiful, hardly glamorous. Too cool, too stubborn. So why was he already imagining her naked and wrapped around him? "What is it between us?"

"Animosity."

He grinned, abruptly and completely charming her. She could have murdered him for it. "Maybe part, but even that's too strong for such a short association. A minute ago I was wondering what it would be like to make love with you. Believe it or not, I don't do that with every woman I meet."

Her palms were damp again. "Am I supposed to be flattered?"

"No. I just figure we'll deal better together if we understand each other."

The need to turn and run was desperate. Too desperate. A.J. held her ground. "Understand this. I represent Clarissa DeBasse. I'll look out for her interests, her welfare. If you try to do anything detrimental to her professionally or personally, I'll cut you off at the knees. Other than that, we really don't have anything to worry about."

"Time will tell."

For the first time she took a step away from him. A.J. didn't consider it a retreat as she walked over and put her hand on the light switch. "I have a breakfast meeting in the morning. Let's get the contracts signed, Brady, so we can both do our jobs."

Chapter Three

Preproduction meetings generally left his staff frazzled and out of sorts. David thrived on them. Lists of figures that insisted on being balanced appealed to the practical side of him. Translating those figures into lights, sets and props challenged his creativity. If he hadn't enjoyed finding ways to merge the two, he never would have chosen to be a producer.

He was a man who had a reputation for knowing his own mind and altering circumstances to suit it. The reputation permeated his professional life and filtered through to the personal. As a producer he was tough and, according to many directors, not always fair. As a man he was generous and, according to many women, not always warm.

David would give a director creative freedom, but only to a point. When the creative freedom tempted the director to veer from David's overall view of a project, he stopped him dead. He would discuss, listen and at times compromise. An astute director would realize that the compromise hadn't affected the producer's wishes in the least.

In a relationship he would give a woman an easy, attentive companion. If a woman preferred roses, there would be roses. If she enjoyed rides in the country, there would be rides in the country. But if she attempted to get beneath the skin, he stopped her dead. He would discuss, listen and at times compromise. An astute woman would realize the compromise hadn't affected the man in the least.

Directors would call him tough, but would grudgingly admit they would work with him again. Women would call him cool, but would smile when they heard his voice over the phone.

Neither of these things came to him through carefully thought out strategy, but simply because he was a man who was careful with his private thoughts—and private needs.

By the time the preproduction meetings were over, the location set and the format gelled, David was anxious for results. He'd picked his team individually, down to the last technician. Because he'd developed a personal interest in Clarissa DeBasse, he decided to begin with her. His choice, he was certain, had nothing to do with her agent.

His initial desire to have her interviewed in her own home was cut off quickly by a brief memo from A. J. Fields. Miss DeBasse was entitled to her privacy. Period. Unwilling to be hampered by a technicality, David arranged for the studio to be decorated in precisely the same homey, suburban atmosphere. He'd have her interviewed there by veteran journalist Alex Marshall. David wanted to thread credibility through speculation. A man of Marshall's reputation could do it for him.

David kept in the background and let his crew take over. He'd had problems with this director before, but both projects they'd collaborated on had won awards. The end product, to David, was the bottom line.

"Put a filter on that light," the director ordered. "We may have to look like we're sitting in the furniture department in the mall, but I want atmosphere. Alex, if you'd run through your intro, I'd like to get a fix on the angle."

"Fine." Reluctantly Alex tapped out his two-dollar cigar and went to work. David checked his watch. Clarissa was late, but not late enough to cause alarm yet. In another ten minutes he'd have an assistant give her a call. He watched Alex run through the intro flawlessly, then wait while the director fussed with the lights. Deciding he wasn't needed at the moment, David opted to make the call himself. Only he'd make it to A.J.'s office. No harm in giving her a hard time, he thought as he pushed through the studio doors. She seemed to be the better for it.

"Oh, David, I do apologize."

He stopped as Clarissa hurried down the hallway. She wasn't anyone's aunt today, he thought, as she reached out to take his hands. Her hair was swept dramatically back, making her look both flamboyant and years younger. There was a necklace of silver links around her neck that held an amethyst the size of his thumb. Her makeup was artfully applied to accent clear blue eyes, just as her dress, deep and rich, accented them. This wasn't the woman who'd fed him meat loaf.

"Clarissa, you look wonderful."

"Thank you. I'm afraid I didn't have much time to prepare. I got the days mixed, you see, and was right in the middle of weeding my petunias when Aurora came to pick me up."

He caught himself looking over her shoulder and down the hall. "She's here?"

"She's parking the car." Clarissa glanced back over her shoulder with a sigh. "I know I'm a trial to her, always have been."

"She doesn't seem to feel that way."

"No, she doesn't. Aurora's so generous."

He'd reserve judgment on that one. "Are you ready, or would you like some coffee or tea first?"

"No, no, I don't like any stimulants when I'm working. They tend to cloud things." Their hands were still linked when her gaze fastened on his. "You're a bit restless, David."

She said it the moment he'd looked back, and had seen A.J. coming down the hall. "I'm always edgy on a shoot," he said absently. Why was it he hadn't noticed how she walked before? Fast and fluid.

"That's not it," Clarissa commented, and patted his hand. "But I won't invade your privacy. Ah, here's Aurora. Should we start?"

"We already have," he murmured, still watching A.J.

"Good morning, David. I hope we haven't thrown you off schedule."

She was as sleek and professional as she'd been the first time he'd seen her. Why was it now that he noticed small details? The collar of her blouse rose high on what he knew was a long, slender neck. Her mouth was unpainted. He wanted to take a step closer to see if she wore the same scent. Instead he took Clarissa's arm. "Not at all. I take it you want to watch."

"Of course."

"Just inside here, Clarissa." He pushed open the door. "I'd like to introduce you to your director, Sam Cauldwell. Sam." It didn't appear to bother David that he was interrupting his director. A.J. noticed that he stood where he was and waited for Cauldwell to come to him. She could hardly censor him for it when she'd have used the same technique herself. "This is Clarissa DeBasse."

Cauldwell stemmed obvious impatience to take her hand. "A pleasure, Miss DeBasse. I read both your books to give myself a feel for your segment of the program."

"That's very kind of you. I hope you enjoyed them."

"I don't know if 'enjoyed' is the right word." He gave a quick shake of his head. "They certainly gave me something to think about."

"Miss DeBasse is ready to start whenever you're set."

"Great. Would you mind taking a seat over here. We'll take a voice test and recheck the lighting."

As Cauldwell led her away, David saw A.J. watching him like a hawk. "You make a habit of hovering over your clients, A.J.?"

Satisfied that Clarissa was all right for the moment, A.J. turned to him. "Yes. Just the way I imagine you hover over your directors."

"All in a day's work, right? You can get a better view from over here."

"Thanks." She moved with him to the left of the studio, watching as Clarissa was introduced to Alex Marshall. The veteran newscaster was tall, lean and distinguished. Twenty-five years in the game had etched a few lines on his face, but the gray threading through his hair contrasted nicely with his deep tan. "A wise choice for your narrator," she commented.

"The face America trusts."

"There's that, of course. Also, I can't imagine him putting up with any nonsense. Bring in a palm reader from Sunset Boulevard and he'll make her look like a fool regardless of the script."

"That's right."

A.J. sent him an even look. "He won't make a fool out of Clarissa."

He gave her a slow, acknowledging nod. "That's what I'm counting on. I called your office last week."

"Yes, I know." A.J. saw Clarissa laugh at something Alex said. "Didn't my assistant get back to you?"

"I didn't want to talk to your assistant."

"I've been tied up. You've very nearly recreated Clarissa's living room, haven't you?"

"That's the idea. You're trying to avoid me, A.J." He shifted just enough to block her view, so that she was forced to look at him. Because he'd annoyed her, she made the look thorough, starting at his shoes, worn canvas high tops, up the casual pleated slacks to the open collar of his shirt before she settled on his face.

"I'd hoped you catch on."

"And you might succeed at it." He ran his finger down her lapel, over a pin of a half-moon. "But she's going to get in the way." He glanced over his shoulder at Clarissa.

She schooled herself for this, lectured herself and rehearsed the right responses. Somehow it wasn't as easy as she'd imagined. "David, you don't seem to be one of those men who are attracted to rejection."

"No." His thumb continued to move over the pin as he looked back at her. "You don't seem to be one of those women who pretend disinterest to attract."

"I don't pretend anything." She looked directly into his eyes, determined not a flicker of her own unease would show. "I am disinterested. And you're standing in my way."

"That's something that might get to be a habit." But he moved aside.

It took nearly another forty-five minutes of discussion, changes and technical fine tuning before they were ready to shoot. Because she was relieved David was busy elsewhere, A.J. waited patiently. Which meant she only checked her watch a half a dozen times. Clarissa sat easily on the sofa and sipped water. But whenever she glanced up and looked in her direction, A.J. was glad she'd decided to come.

The shoot began well enough. Clarissa sat with Alex on the sofa. He asked questions; she answered. They touched on clairvoyance, precognition, Clarissa's interest in astrology. Clarissa had a knack for taking long, confusing phrases and making them simple, understandable. One of the reasons she was often in demand on the lecture circuit was her ability to take the mysteries of Psi and relate them to the average person. It was one area A.J. could be certain Clarissa DeBasse would handle herself. Relaxing, she took a piece of hard candy out of her briefcase in lieu of lunch.

They shot, reshot, altered angles and repeated them-
selves for the camera. Hours passed, but A.J. was content.
Quality was the order of day. She wanted nothing less for
Clarissa.

Then they brought out the cards.

She'd nearly taken a step forward, when the slightest signal from Clarissa had her fuming and staying where she
was. She hated this, and always had.

"Problem?"

She hadn't realized he'd come up beside her. A.J. sent
David a killing look before she riveted her attention on the
set again. "We didn't discuss anything like this."

"The cards?" Surprised by her response, David, too,
watched the set. "We cleared it with Clarissa."

A.J. set her teeth. "Next time, Brady, clear it with me."

David decided that whatever nasty retort he could make
would wait when Alex's broadcaster's voice rose rich and
clear in the studio. "Miss DeBasse, using cards to test ESP
is a rather standard device, isn't it?"

"A rather limited test, yes. They're also an aid in testing
telepathy."

"You've been involved in testing of this sort before, at
Stanford, UCLA, Columbia, Duke, as well as institutions
in England."

"Yes, I have."

"Would you mind explaining the process?"

"Of course. The cards used in laboratory tests are generally two colors, with perhaps five different shapes.
Squares, circles, wavy lines, that sort of thing. Using these,
it's possible to determine chance and what goes beyond
chance. That is, with two colors, it's naturally a fifty-fifty
proposition. If a subject hits the colors fifty percent of the
time, it's accepted as chance. If a subject hits sixty percent,
then it's ten percent over chance."

"It sounds relatively simple."

"With colors alone, yes. The shapes alter that. With say, twenty-five cards in a run, the tester is able to determine by the number of hits, or correct answers, how much over chance the subject guessed. If the subject hits fifteen times out of twenty-five, it can be assumed the subject's ESP abilities are highly tuned."

"She's very good," David murmured.

"Damned right she is." A.J. folded her arms and tried not to be annoyed. This was Clarissa's business, and no one knew it better.

"Could you explain how it works—for you, that is?" Alex idly shuffled the pack of cards as he spoke to her. "Do you get a feeling when a card is held up?"

"A picture," Clarissa corrected. "One gets a picture."

"Are you saying you get an actual picture of the card?"

"An actual picture can be held in your hand." She smiled at him patiently. "I'm sure you read a great deal, Mr. Marshall."

"Yes, I do."

"When you read, the words, the phrasings make pictures in your head. This is very similar to that."

"I see." His doubt was obvious, and to David, the perfect reaction. "That's imagination."

"ESP requires a control of the imagination and a sharpening of concentration."

"Can anyone do this?"

"That's something that's still being researched. There are some who feel ESP can be learned. Others believe psychics are born. My own opinion falls in between."

"Can you explain?"

"I think every one of us has certain talents or abilities, and the degree to which they're developed and used depends on the individual. It's possible to block these abilities. It's more usual, I think, to simply ignore them so that they never come into question."

"Your abilities have been documented. We'd like to give an impromptu demonstration here, with your cooperation."

"Of course."

"This is an ordinary deck of playing cards. One of the crew purchased them this morning, and you haven't handled them. Is that right?"

"No, I haven't. I'm not very clever with games." She smiled, half apologetic, half amused, and delighted the director.

"Now if I pick a card and hold it like this." Alex pulled one from the middle of the deck and held its back to her. "Can you tell me what it is?"

"No." Her smile never faded as the director started to signal to stop the tape. "You'll have to look at the card, Mr. Marshall, think of it, actually try to picture it in your mind." As the tape continued to roll, Alex nodded and obliged her. "I'm afraid you're not concentrating very hard, but it's a red card. That's better." She beamed at him. "Nine of diamonds."

The camera caught the surprise on his face before he turned the card over. Nine of diamonds. He pulled a second card and repeated the process. When they reached the third, Clarissa stopped, frowning.

"You're trying to confuse me by thinking of a card other than the one in your hand. It blurs things a bit, but the ten of clubs comes through stronger."

"Fascinating," Alex murmured as he turned over the ten of clubs. "Really fascinating."

"I'm afraid this sort of thing is often no more than a parlor game," Clarissa corrected. "A clever mentalist can do nearly the same thing—in a different way, of course."

"You're saying it's a trick."

"I'm saying it can be. I'm not good at tricks myself, so I don't try them, but I can appreciate a good show."

"You started your career by reading palms." Alex set down the cards, not entirely sure of himself.

"A long time ago. Technically anyone can read a palm, interpret the lines." She held hers out to him. "Lines that represent finance, emotion, length of life. A good book out of the library will tell you exactly what to look for and how to find it. A sensitive doesn't actually read a palm so much as absorb feelings."

Charmed, but far from sold, Alex held out his. "I don't quite see how you could absorb feelings by looking at the palm of my hand."

"You transmit them," she told him. "Just as you transmit everything else, your hopes, your sorrows, your joys. I can take your palm and at a glance tell you that you communicate well and have a solid financial base, but that would hardly be earth-shattering news. But..." She held her own out to him. "If you don't mind," she began, and cupped his hand in hers. "I can look again and say that—" She stopped, blinked and stared at him. "Oh."

A.J. made a move forward, only to be blocked by David. "Let her be," he muttered. "This is a documentary, remember. We can't have it staged and tidy. If she's uncomfortable with this part of the tape we can cut it."

"If she's uncomfortable you will cut it."

Clarissa's hand was smooth and firm under Alex's, but her eyes were wide and stunned. "Should I be nervous?" he asked, only half joking.

"Oh, no." With a little laugh, she cleared her throat. "No, not at all. You have very strong vibrations, Mr. Marshall."

"Thank you. I think."

"You're a widower, fifteen, sixteen years now. You were a very good husband." She smiled at him, relaxed again. "You can be proud of that. And a good father."

"I appreciate that, Miss DeBasse, but again, it's hardly news."

She continued as if he hadn't spoken. "Both your children are settled now, which eases your mind, as it does any parent's. They never gave you a great deal of worry, though there was a period with your son, during his early twenties, when you had some rough spots. But some people take longer to find their niche, don't they?"

He wasn't smiling anymore, but staring at her as intensely as she stared at him. "I suppose."

"You're a perfectionist, in your work and in your private life. That made it a little difficult for your son. He couldn't quite live up to your expectations. You shouldn't have worried so much, but of course all parents do. Now that he's going to be a father himself, you're closer. The idea of grandchildren pleases you. At the same time it makes you think more about the future—your own mortality. But I wonder if you're wise to be thinking of retiring. You're in the prime of your life and too used to deadlines and rushing to be content with that fishing boat for very long. Now if you'd—" She stopped herself with a little shake of the head. "I'm sorry. I tend to ramble on when someone interests me. I'm always afraid of getting too personal."

"Not at all." He closed his hand into a loose fist. "Miss DeBasse, you're quite amazing."

"Cut!" Cauldwell could have gotten down on his knees and kissed Clarissa's feet. Alex Marshall considering retirement. There hadn't been so much as a murmur of it on the grapevine. "I want to see the playback in thirty minutes. Alex, thank you. It's a great start. Miss DeBasse—" He'd have taken her hand again if he hadn't been a little leery of giving off the wrong vibrations. "You were sensational. I can't wait to start the next segment with you."

Before he'd finished thanking her, A.J. was at her side. She knew what would happen, what invariably happened.

One of the crew would come up and tell Clarissa about a "funny thing that happened to him." Then there would be another asking for his palm to be read. Some would be smirking, others would be curious, but inside of ten minutes Clarissa would be surrounded.

"If you're ready, I'll drive you home," A.J. began.

"Now I thought we'd settled that." Clarissa looked idly around for her purse without any idea where she'd set it. "It's too far for you to drive all the way to Newport Beach and back again."

"Just part of the service." A.J. handed her the purse she'd been holding throughout the shoot.

"Oh, thank you, dear. I couldn't imagine what I'd done with it. I'll take a cab."

"We have a driver for you." David didn't have to look at A.J. to know she was steaming. He could all but feel the heat. "We wouldn't dream of having you take a cab all the way back."

"That's very kind."

"But it won't be necessary," A.J. put in.

"No, it won't." Smoothly Alex edged in and took Clarissa's hand. "I'm hoping Miss DeBasse will allow me to drive her home—after she has dinner with me."

"That would be lovely," Clarissa told him before A.J. could say a word. "I hope I didn't embarrass you, Mr. Marshall."

"Not at all. In fact, I was fascinated."

"How nice. Thank you for staying with me, dear." She kissed A.J.'s cheek. "It always puts me at ease. Good night, David."

"Good night, Clarissa. Alex." He stood beside A.J. as they linked arms and strolled out of the studio. "A nice-looking couple."

Before the words were out of his mouth, A.J. turned on him. If it had been possible to grow fangs, she'd have grown them. "You jerk." She was halfway to the studio doors before he stopped her.

"And what's eating you?"

If he hadn't said it with a smile on his face, she might have controlled herself. "I want to see that last fifteen minutes of tape, Brady, and if I don't like what I see, it's out."

"I don't recall anything in the contract about you having editing rights, A.J."

"There's nothing in the contract saying that Clarissa would read palms, either."

"Granted. Alex ad-libbed that, and it worked very well. What's the problem?"

"You were watching, damn it." Needing to turn her temper on something, she rammed through the studio doors.

"I was," David agreed as he took her arm to slow her down. "But obviously I didn't see what you did."

"She was covering." A.J. raked a hand through her hair. "She felt something as soon as she took his hand. When you look at the tape you'll see five, ten seconds where she just stares."

"So it adds to the mystique. It's effective."

"Damn your 'effective'!" She swung around so quickly she nearly knocked him into a wall. "I don't like to see her hit that way. I happen to care about her as a person, not just a commodity."

"All right, hold it. Hold it!" He caught up to her again as she shoved through the outside door. "There didn't seem to be a thing wrong with Clarissa when she left here."

"I don't like it." A.J. stormed down the steps toward the parking lot. "First the lousy cards. I'm sick of seeing her tested that way."

"A.J., the cards are a natural. She's done that same test, in much greater intensity, for institutes all over the country."

"I know. And it makes me furious that she has to prove herself over and over. Then that palm business. Something upset her." She began to pace on the patch of lawn bordering the sidewalk. "There was something there and I didn't even have the chance to talk to her about it before that six-foot reporter with the golden voice muscled in."

"Alex?" Though he tried, for at least five seconds, to control himself, David roared with laughter. "God, you're priceless."

Her eyes narrowed, her face paled with rage, she stopped pacing. "So you think it's funny, do you? A trusting, amazingly innocent woman goes off with a virtual stranger and you laugh. If anything happens to her—"

"Happens?" David rolled his eyes skyward. "Good God, A.J., Alex Marshall is hardly a maniac. He's a highly respected member of the news media. And Clarissa is certainly old enough to make up her own mind—and make her own dates."

"It's not a date."

"Looked that way to me."

She opened her mouth, shut it again, then whirled around toward the parking lot.

"Now wait a minute. I said wait." He took her by both arms and trapped her between himself and a parked car. "I'll be damned if I'm going to chase you all over L.A."

"Just go back inside and take a look at that take. I want to see it tomorrow."

"I don't take orders from paranoid agents or anyone else. We're going to settle this right here. I don't know what's working on you, A.J., but I can't believe you're this upset because a client's going out to dinner."

"She's not just a client," A.J. hurled back at him. "She's my mother."

Her furious announcement left them both momentarily speechless. He continued to hold her by the shoulders while she fought to even her breathing. Of course he should have seen it, David realized. The shape of the face, the eyes. Especially the eyes. "I'll be damned."

"I can only second that," she murmured, then let herself lean back against the car. "Look, that's not for publication. Understand?"

"Why?"

"Because we both prefer it that way. Our relationship is private."

"All right." He rarely argued with privacy. "Okay, that explains why you take such a personal interest, but I think you carry it a bit too far."

"I don't care what you think." Because her head was beginning to pound, she straightened. "Excuse me."

"No." Calmly David blocked her way. "Some people might say you interfere with your mother's life because you don't have enough to fill your own."

Her eyes became very dark, her skin very pale. "My life is none of your business, Brady."

"Not at the moment, but while this project's going on, Clarissa's is. Give her some room, A.J."

Because it sounded so reasonable, her hackles rose. "You don't understand."

"No, maybe you should explain it to me."

"What if Alex Marshall presses her for an interview over dinner? What if he wants to get her alone so he can hammer at her?"

"What if he simply wanted to have dinner with an interesting, attractive woman? You might give Clarissa more credit."

She folded her arms. "I won't have her hurt."

He could argue with her. He could even try reason. Somehow he didn't think either would work quite yet. "Let's go for a drive."

"What?"

"A drive. You and me." He smiled at her. "It happens to be my car you're leaning on."

"Oh, sorry." She straightened again. "I have to get back to the office. There's some paperwork I let hang today."

"Then it can hang until tomorrow." Drawing out his keys, he unlocked the door. "I could use a ride along the beach."

So could she. She'd overreacted—there was no question of it. She needed some air, some speed, something to clear her head. Maybe it wasn't wise to take it with him, but... "Are you going to put the top down?"

"Absolutely."

It helped—the drive, the air, the smell of the sea, the blare of the radio. He didn't chat at her or try to ease her into conversation. A.J. did something she allowed herself to do rarely in the company of others. She relaxed.

How long had it been, she wondered, since she'd driven along the coast, no time frame, no destination? If she couldn't remember, then it had been too long. A.J. closed her eyes, emptied her mind and enjoyed.

Just who was she? David asked himself as he watched her relax, degree by degree, beside him. Was she the tough, nononsense agent with an eye out for ten percent of a smooth deal? Was she the fiercely protective, obviously devoted daughter—who was raking in that same ten percent of her mother's talent on one hand and raising the roof about exploitation the next. He couldn't figure her.

He was a good judge of people. In his business he'd be producing home movies if he weren't. Yet when he'd kissed her he hadn't found the hard-edged, self-confident woman he'd expected, but a nervous, vulnerable one. For some reason, she didn't entirely fit who she was, or what she'd chosen to be. It might be interesting to find out why.

"Hungry?"

Half dreaming, A.J. opened her eyes and looked at him. How was it he hadn't seen it before? David asked himself. The eyes, the eyes were so like Clarissa's, the shape, the color, the... depth, he decided for lack of a better word. It ran through his head that maybe she was like Clarissa in other ways. Then he dismissed it.

"I'm sorry," she murmured, "I wasn't paying attention." But she could have described his face in minute detail, from the hard cheekbones to the slight indentation in his chin. Letting out a long breath, she drew herself in. A wise woman controlled her thoughts as meticulously as her emotions.

"I asked if you were hungry."

"Yes." She stretched her shoulders. "How far have we gone?"

Not far enough. The thought ran unbidden through his mind. Not nearly far enough. "About twenty miles. Your choice." He eased over to the shoulder of the road and indicated a restaurant on one side and a hamburger stand on the other."

"I'll take the burger. If we can sit on the beach."

"Nothing I like better than a cheap date."

A.J. let herself out. "This isn't a date."

"I forgot. You can pay for your own." He'd never heard her laugh like that before. Easy, feminine, fresh. "Just for that I'll spring." But he didn't touch her as they walked up to the stand. "What'll it be?"

"The jumbo burger, large fries and the super shake. Chocolate."

"Big talk."

As they waited, they watched a few early evening swimmers splash in the shallows. Gulls swooped around, chattering and loitering near the stand, waiting for handouts. David left them disappointed as he gathered up the paper bags. "Where to?"

"Down there. I like to watch." A.J. walked out on the beach and, ignoring her linen skirt, dropped down on the sand. "I don't get to the beach often enough." Kicking off her shoes, she slid stockinged feet in the sand so that her skirt hiked up to her thighs. David took a good long look before he settled beside her.

"Neither do I," he decided, wondering just how those legs—and the rest of her—might look in a bikini.

"I guess I made quite a scene."

"I guess you did." He pulled out her hamburger and handed it to her.

"I hate to," she said, and took a fierce bite. "I don't have a reputation as an abrasive or argumentative agent, just a tough one. I only lose objectivity with Clarissa."

He screwed the paper cups into the sand. "Objectivity is shot to hell when we love somebody."

"She's so good. I don't just mean at what she does, but inside." A.J. took the fries he offered and nibbled one. "Good people can get hurt so much easier than others, you know. And she's so willing to give of herself. If she gave everything she wanted, she'd have nothing left."

"So you're there to protect her."

"That's right." She turned, challenging.

"I'm not arguing with you." He held up a hand. "For some reason I'd like to understand."

With a little laugh she looked back out to sea. "You had to be there."

"Why don't you tell me what it was like? Growing up."

She never discussed it with anyone. Then again, she never sat on a beach eating hamburgers with associates. Maybe it was a day for firsts. "She was a wonderful mother. Is. Clarissa's so loving, so generous."

"Your father?"

"He died when I was eight. He was a salesman, so he was away a lot. He was a good salesman," she added with the ghost of a smile. "We were lucky there. There were savings and a little bit of stock. Problem was the bills didn't get paid. Not that the money wasn't there. Clarissa just forgot. You'd pick up the phone and it would be dead because she'd misplaced the bill. I guess I just started taking care of her."

"You'd have been awfully young for that."

"I didn't mind." This time the smile bloomed fully. There were, as with her mother, the faintest of dimples in her cheeks. "I was so much better at managing than she. We had a little more coming in once she started reading palms and doing charts. She really just sort of blossomed then. She has a need to help people, to give them—I don't know—reassurance. Hope. Still, it was an odd time. We lived in a nice neighborhood and people would come and go through our living room. The neighbors were fascinated, and some of them came in regularly for readings, but outside the house there was a kind of distance. It was as if they weren't quite sure of Clarissa."

"It would have been uncomfortable for you."

"Now and then. She was doing what she had to do. Some people shied away from us, from the house, but she never seemed to notice. Anyway, the word spread and she became friends with the Van Camps. I guess I was around twelve or thirteen. The first time movie stars showed up at the house I was awestruck. Within a year it became a matter of course. I've known actors to call her before they'd accept a role. She'd always tell them the same thing. They had to rely on their own feelings. The one thing Clarissa will never do is make decisions for anyone else. But they still called. Then the little Van Camp boy was kidnapped. After that the press camped on the lawn, the phone never stopped. I ended up moving her out to Newport Beach. She can keep a low profile there, even when another case comes up."

"There was the Ridehour murders."

She stood up abruptly and walked closer to the sea. Rising, David walked with her. "You've no idea how she suffered through that." Emotions trembled in her voice as she wrapped her arms around herself. "You can't imagine what a toll something like that can take on a person like Clarissa. I wanted to stop her, but I knew I couldn't."

When she closed her eyes, David put a hand on her shoulder. "Why would you want to stop her if she could help?"

"She grieved. She hurt. God, she all but lived it, even before she was called in." She opened her eyes and turned to him then. "Do you understand, even before she was called in, she was involved."

"I'm not sure I do."

"No, you can't." She gave an impatient shake of her head for expecting it. "I suppose you have to live it. In any case, they asked for help. It doesn't take any more than that with Clarissa. Five young girls dead." She closed her eyes again. "She never speaks of it, but I know she saw each one. I know." Then she pushed the thought aside, as she knew she had to. "Clarissa thinks of her abilities as a gift...but you've no idea what a curse that can be."

"You'd like her to stop. Shut down. Is that possible?"

A.J. laughed again and drew both hands through hair the wind had tossed. "Oh, yes, but not for Clarissa. I've accepted that she needs to give. I just make damn sure the wrong person doesn't take."

"And what about you?" He would have sworn something in her froze at the casual question. "Did you become an agent to protect your mother?"

She relaxed again. "Partly. But I enjoy what I do." Her eyes were clear again. "I'm good at it."

"And what about Aurora?" He brought his hands up her arms to her shoulders.

A yearning rose up in her, just from the touch. She blocked it off. "Aurora's only there for Clarissa."

"Why?"

"Because I know how to protect myself as well as my mother."

"From what?"

"It's getting late, David."

"Yeah." One hand skimmed over to her throat. Her skin was soft there, sun kissed and soft. "I'm beginning to think the same thing. I never did finish kissing you, Aurora."

His hands were strong. She'd noticed it before, but it seemed to matter more now. "It's better that way."

"I'm beginning to think that, too. Damn if I can figure out why I want to so much."

"Give it a little time. It'll pass."

"Why don't we test it out?" He lifted a brow as he looked down at her. "We're on a public beach. The sun hasn't set. If I kiss you here, it can't go any further than that, and maybe we'll figure out why we unnerve each other." When he drew her closer, she stiffened. "Afraid?" Why would the fact that she might be, just a little, arouse him?

"No." Because she'd prepared herself she almost believed it was true. He wouldn't have the upper hand this time, she told herself. She wouldn't allow it. Deliberately she lifted her arms and twined them around his neck. When he hesitated, she pressed her lips to his.

He'd have sworn the sand shifted under his feet. He was certain the crash of the waves grew in volume until it filled the air like thunder. He'd intended to control the situation like an experiment. But intentions changed as mouth met mouth. She tasted warm—cool, sweet—pungent. He had a desperate need to find out which of his senses could be trusted. Before either of them was prepared, he plunged himself into the kiss and dragged her with him.

Too fast. Her mind whirled with the thought. Too far. But her body ignored the warning and strained against him. She wanted, and the want was clearer and sharper than any want had ever been. She needed, and the need was deeper and more intense than any other need. As the feelings drummed into her, her fingers curled into his hair. Hunger for him rose so quickly she moaned with it. It wasn't right. It couldn't be right. Yet the feeling swirled through her that was exactly right and had always been.

A gull swooped overhead and was gone, leaving only the flicker of a shadow, the echo of a sound.

When they drew apart, A.J. stepped back. With distance came a chill, but she welcomed it after the enervating heat. She would have turned then without a word, but his hands were on her again.

"Come home with me."

She had to look at him then. Passion, barely controlled, darkened his eyes. Desire, edged with temptation, roughened his voice. And she felt...too much. If she went, she would give too much.

"No." Her voice wasn't quite steady, but it was final. "I don't want this, David."

"Neither do I." He backed off then. He hadn't meant for things to go so far. He hadn't wanted to feel so much. "I'm not sure that's going to make any difference."

"We have control over our own lives." When she looked out to sea again, the wind rushed her hair back, leaving her face unframed. "I know what I want and don't want in mine."

"Wants change." Why was he arguing? She said nothing he hadn't thought himself.

"Only if we let them."

"And if I said I wanted you?"

The pulse in her throat beat quickly, so quickly she wasn't sure she could get the words around it. "I'd say you were making a mistake. You were right, David, when you said I wasn't your type. Go with your first impulse. It's usually the best.''

"In this case I think I need more data.''

"Suit yourself,'' she said as though it made no difference. "I have to get back. I want to call Clarissa and make sure she's all right.''

He took her arm one last time. "You won't always be able to use her, Aurora.''

She stopped and sent him the cool, intimate look so like her mother's. "I don't use her at all,'' she murmured. "That's the difference between us.'' She turned and made her way back across the sand.

Chapter Four

There was moonlight, shafts of it, glimmering. There was the scent of hyacinths—the faintest fragrance on the faintest of breezes. From somewhere came the sound of water, running, bubbling. On a wide-planked wood floor there were shadows, the shifting grace of an oak outside the window. A painting on the wall caught the eye and held it. It was no more than slashes of red and violet lines on a white, white canvas, but somehow it portrayed energy, movement, tensions with undercurrents of sex. There was a mirror, taller than most. A.J. saw herself reflected in it.

She looked indistinct, ethereal, lost. With shadows all around it seemed to her she could just step forward into the glass and be gone. The chill that went through her came not from without but from within. There was something to fear here, something as nebulous as her own reflection. Instinct told her to go, and to go quickly, before she learned what it was. But as she turned something blocked her way.

David stood between her and escape, his hands firm on her shoulders. When she looked at him she saw that his eyes were dark and impatient. Desire—his or hers—thickened the air until even breathing was an effort.

I don't want this. Did she say it? Did she simply think it? Though she couldn't be sure, she heard his response clearly enough, clipped and annoyed.

"You can't keep running, Aurora. Not from me, not from yourself."

Then she was sliding down into a dark, dark tunnel with soft edges just beginning to flame.

A.J. jerked up in bed, breathless and trembling. She didn't see moonlight, but the first early shafts of sun coming through her own bedroom windows. Her bedroom, she repeated to herself as she pushed sleep-tousled hair from her eyes. There were no hyacinths here, no shadows, no disturbing painting.

A dream, she repeated over and over. It had just been a dream. But why did it have to be so real? She could almost feel the slight pressure on her shoulders where his hands had pressed. The turbulent, churning sensation through her system hadn't faded. And why had she dreamed of David Brady?

There were several logical reasons she could comfort herself with. He'd been on her mind for the past couple of weeks. Clarissa and the documentary had been on her mind and they were all tangled together. She'd been working hard, maybe too hard, and the last true relaxation she'd had, had been those few minutes with him on the beach.

Still, it was best not to think of that, of what had happened or nearly happened, of what had been said or left unsaid. It would be better, much better, to think of schedules, of work and of obligations.

There'd be no sleeping now. Though it was barely six, A.J. pushed the covers aside and rose. A couple of strong cups of black coffee and a cool shower would put her back in order. They had to. Her schedule was much too busy to allow her to waste time worrying over a dream.

Her kitchen was spacious and very organized. She allowed no clutter, even in a room she spent little time in. Counters and appliances gleamed in stark white, as much from the diligence of her housekeeper as from disuse. A.J. went down the two steps that separated the kitchen from the living area and headed for the appliance she knew best. The coffee maker.

Turning off the automatic alarm, which would have begun the brewing at 7:05, A.J. switched it to Start. When she came out of the shower fifteen minutes later, the scent of coffee—of normalcy—was back. She drank the first cup black, for the caffeine rather than the taste. Though she was an hour ahead of schedule, A.J. stuck to routine. Nothing as foolish and insubstantial as a dream was going to throw her off. She downed a handful of vitamins, preferring them to hassling with breakfast, then took a second cup of coffee into the bedroom with her to dress. As she studied the contents of her closet, she reviewed her appointments for the day.

Brunch with a very successful, very nervous client who was being wooed for a prime-time series. It wouldn't hurt to look over the script for the pilot once more before they discussed it. A prelunch staff meeting in her own conference room was next. Then there was a late business lunch with Bob Hopewell, who'd begun casting his new feature. She had two clients she felt were tailor-made for the leads. After mentally reviewing her appointments, A.J. decided what she needed was a touch of elegance.

She went with a raw silk suit in pale peach. Sticking to routine, she was dressed and standing in front of the full-length mirrors of her closet in twenty minutes. As an afterthought, she picked up the little half-moon she sometimes wore on her lapel. As she was fastening it, the dream came back to her. She hadn't looked so confident, so—was it aloof—in the dream. She'd been softer, hadn't she? More vulnerable.

A.J. lifted a hand to touch it to the glass. It was cool and smooth, a reflection only. Just as it had only been a dream, she reminded herself with a shake of the head. In reality she couldn't afford to be soft. Vulnerability was out of the question. An agent in this town would be eaten alive in five minutes if she allowed a soft spot to show. And a woman— a woman took terrifying chances if she let a man see that which was vulnerable. A. J. Fields wasn't taking any chances.

Tugging down the hem of her jacket, she took a last survey before grabbing her briefcase. In less than twenty minutes, she was unlocking the door to her suite of offices.

It wasn't an unusual occurrence for A.J. to open the offices herself. Ever since she'd rented her first one-room walk-up early in her career, she'd developed the habit of arriving ahead of her staff. In those days her staff had consisted of a part-time receptionist who'd dreamed of a modeling career. Now she had two receptionists, a secretary and an assistant, as well as a stable of agents. A.J. turned the switch so that light gleamed on brass pots and rose-colored walls. She'd never regretted calling in a decorator. There was class here, discreet, understated class with subtle hints of power. Left to herself, she knew she'd have settled for a couple of sturdy desks and goose-neck lamps.

A glance at her watch showed her she could get in several calls to the East Coast. She left the one light burning in the reception area and closeted herself in her own office. Within a half-hour she'd verbally agreed to have her nervous brunch appointment fly east to do a pilot for a weekly series, set out prenegotiation feelers for a contract renewal for another client who worked on a daytime drama and lit a fire under a producer by refusing his offer on a projected mini-series.

A good morning's work, A.J. decided, reflecting back on the producer's assessment that she was a nearsighted, money-grubbing python. He would counteroffer. She leaned back in her chair and let her shoes drop to the floor. When he did, her client would get over-the-title billing and a cool quarter million. He'd work for it, A.J. thought with a long stretch. She'd read the script and understood that the part would be physically demanding and emotionally draining. She understood just how much blood and sweat a good actor put into a role. As far as she was concerned, they deserved every penny they could get, and it was up to her to squeeze it from the producer's tightfisted hand.

Satisfied, she decided to delve into paperwork before her own phone started to ring. Then she heard the footsteps.

At first she simply glanced at her watch, wondering who was in early. Then it occurred to her that though her staff was certainly dedicated enough, she couldn't think of anyone who'd come to work thirty minutes before they were due. A.J. rose, fully intending to see for herself, when the footsteps stopped. She should just call out, she thought, then found herself remembering every suspense movie she'd ever seen. The trusting heroine called out, then found herself trapped in a room with a maniac. Swallowing, she picked up a heavy metal paperweight.

The footsteps started again, coming closer. Still closer. Struggling to keep her breathing even and quiet, A.J. walked across the carpet and stood beside the door. The footsteps halted directly on the other side. With the paperweight held high, she put her hand on the knob, held her breath, then yanked it open. David managed to grab her wrist before she knocked him out cold.

"Always greet clients this way, A.J.?"

"Damn it!" She let the paperweight slip to the floor as relief flooded through her. "You scared me to death, Brady. What are you doing sneaking around here at this hour?"

"The same thing you're doing sneaking around here at this hour. I got up early."

Because her knees were shaking, she gave into the urge to sit, heavily. "The difference is this is *my* office. I can sneak around anytime I like. What do you want?"

"I could claim I couldn't stay away from your sparkling personality."

"Cut it."

"The truth is I have to fly to New York for a location shoot. I'll be tied up for a couple of days and wanted you to pass a message on to Clarissa for me." It wasn't the truth at all, but he didn't mind lying. It was easier to swallow than the fact that he'd needed to see her again. He'd woken up that morning knowing he had to see her before he left. Admit that to a woman like A. J. Fields and she'd either run like hell or toss you out.

"Fine." She was already up and reaching for a pad. "I'll be glad to pass on a message. But next time try to remember some people shoot other people who wander into places before hours."

"The door was unlocked," he pointed out. "There was no one at reception, so I decided to see if anyone was around before I just left a note."

It sounded reasonable. Was reasonable. But it didn't suit A.J. to be scared out of her wits before 9:00 a.m. "What's the message, Brady?"

He didn't have the vaguest idea. Tucking his hands in his pockets, he glanced around her meticulously ordered, pastel-toned office. "Nice place," he commented. He noticed even the papers she'd obviously been working with on her desk were in neat piles. There wasn't so much as a paper clip out of place. "You're a tidy creature, aren't you?"

"Yes." She tapped the pencil impatiently on the pad. "The message for Clarissa?"

"How is she, by the way?"

"She's fine."

He took a moment to stroll over to study the single painting she had on the wall. A seascape, very tranquil and soothing. "I remember you were concerned about her—about her having dinner with Alex."

"She had a lovely time," A.J. mumbled. "She told me Alex Marshall was a complete gentleman with a fascinating mind."

"Does that bother you?"

"Clarissa doesn't see men. Not that way." Feeling foolish, she dropped the pad on her desk and walked to her window.

"Is something wrong with her seeing men. That way?"

"No, no, of course not. It's just..."

"Just what, Aurora?"

She shouldn't be discussing her mother, but so few people knew of their relationship, A.J. opened up before she could stop herself. "She gets sort of breathy and vague whenever she mentions him. They spent the day together on Sunday. On his boat. I don't remember Clarissa ever stepping foot on a boat."

"So she's trying something new."

"That's what I'm afraid of," she said under her breath. "Have you any idea what it's like to see your mother in the first stages of infatuation?"

"No." He thought of his own mother's comfortable relationship with his father. She cooked dinner and sewed his buttons. He took out the trash and fixed the toaster. "I can't say I have."

"Well, it's not the most comfortable feeling, I can tell you. What do I know about this man, anyway? Oh, he's smooth," she muttered. "For all I know he's been smooth with half the women in Southern California."

"Do you hear yourself?" Half-amused, David joined her at the window. "You sound like a mother fussing over her teenage daughter. If Clarissa were an ordinary middle-aged woman there'd be little enough to worry about. Don't you think the fact that she is what she is gives her an advantage? It seems she'd be an excellent judge of character."

"You don't understand. Emotions can block things, especially when it's important."

"If that's true, maybe you should look to your own emotions." He felt her freeze. He didn't have to touch her; he didn't have to move any closer. He simply felt it. "You're letting your affection and concern for your mother cause you to overreact to a very simple thing. Maybe you should give some thought to targeting some of that emotion elsewhere."

"Clarissa's all I can afford to be emotional about."

"An odd way of phrasing things. Do you ever give any thought to your own needs? Emotional," he murmured, then ran a hand down her hair. "Physical."

"That's none of your business." She would have turned away, but he kept his hand on her hair.

"You can cut a lot of people off." He felt the first edge of her anger as she stared up at him. Oddly he enjoyed it. "I think you'd be extremely good at picking up the spear and jabbing men out of your way. But it won't work with me."

"I don't know why I thought I could talk to you."

"But you did. That should give you something to consider."

"Why are you pushing me?" she demanded. Fire came into her eyes. She remembered the dream too clearly. The dream, the desire, the fears.

"Because I want you." He stood close, close enough for her scent to twine around him. Close enough so that the doubts and distrust in her eyes were very clear. "I want to make love with you for a long, long time in a very quiet place. When we're finished I might find out why I don't seem to be able to sleep for dreaming of it."

Her throat was dry enough to ache and her hands felt like ice. "I told you once I don't sleep around."

"That's good," he murmured. "That's very good, because I don't think either of us needs a lot of comparisons." He heard the sound of the front door of the offices opening. "Sounds like you're open for business, A.J. Just one more personal note. I'm willing to negotiate terms, times and places, but the bottom line is that I'm going to spend more than one night with you. Give it some thought."

A.J. conquered the urge to pick up the paperweight and heave it at him as he walked to the door. Instead she reminded herself that she was a professional and it was business hours. "Brady."

He turned, and with a hand on the knob smiled at her. "Yeah, Fields?"

"You never gave me the message for Clarissa."

"Didn't I?" The hell with the gingerbread, he decided. "Give her my best. See you around, lady."

David didn't even know what time it was when he unlocked the door of his hotel suite. The two-day shoot had stretched into three. Now all he had to do was figure out which threads to cut and remain in budget. Per instructions, the maid hadn't touched the stacks and piles of paper on the table in the parlor. They were as he'd left them, a chaotic jumble of balance sheets, schedules and production notes.

After a twelve-hour day, he'd ordered his crew to hit the sheets. David buzzed room service and ordered a pot of coffee before he sat down and began to work. After two hours, he was satisfied enough with the figures to go back over the two and a half days of taping.

The Danjason Institute of Parapsychology itself had been impressive, and oddly stuffy, in the way of institutes. It was difficult to imagine that an organization devoted to the study of bending spoons by will and telepathy could be stuffy. The team of parapsychologists they'd worked with had been as dry and precise as any staff of scientists. So dry, in fact, David wondered whether they'd convince the audience or simply put them to sleep. He'd have to supervise the editing carefully.

The testing had been interesting enough, he decided. The fact that they used not only sensitives but people more or less off the street. The testing and conclusions were done in the strictest scientific manner. How had it been put? The application of math probability theory to massive accumulation of data. It sounded formal and supercilious. To David it was card guessing.

Still, put sophisticated equipment and intelligent, highly educated scientists together, and it was understood that psychic phenomena were being researched seriously and intensely. It was, as a science, just beginning to be recognized after decades of slow, exhaustive experimentation.

Then there had been the interview on Wall Street with the thirty-two-year-old stockbroker-psychic. David let out a stream of smoke and watched it float toward the ceiling as he let that particular segment play in his mind. The man had made no secret of the fact that he used his abilities to play the market and become many times a millionaire. It was a skill, he'd explained, much like reading, writing and calculating were skills. He'd also claimed that several top executives in some of the most powerful companies in the world had used psychic powers to get there and to stay there. He'd described ESP as a tool, as important in the business world as a computer system or a slide rule.

A science, a business and a performance.

It made David think of Clarissa. She hadn't tossed around confusing technology or littered her speech with mathematical probabilities. She hadn't discussed market trends or the Dow Jones Average. She'd simply talked, person to person. Whatever powers she had . . .

With a shake of his head, David cut himself off. Listen to this, he thought as he ran his hands over his face. He was beginning to buy the whole business himself, though he knew from his own research that for every lab-contained experiment there were dozens of card-wielding, bell-ringing charlatans bilking a gullible audience. He drew smoke down an already raw throat before he crushed out the cigarette. If he didn't continue to look at the documentary objectively, he'd have a biased mess on his hands.

But even looking objectively, he could see Clarissa as the center of the work. She could be the hinge on which everything else hung. With his eyes half-closed, David could picture it—the interview with the somber-eyed, white-coated parapsychologists, with their no-nonsense laboratory conditions. Then a cut to Clarissa talking with Alex, covering more or less the same ground in her simpler style. Then there'd be the clip of the stockbroker in his sky-high Wall Street office, then back to Clarissa again, seated on the homey sofa. He'd have the tuxedoed mentalist they'd lined up in Vegas doing his flashy, fast-paced demonstration. Then Clarissa again, calmly identifying cards without looking at them. Contrasts, angles, information, but everything would lead back to Clarissa DeBasse. She was the hook—instinct, intuition or paranormal powers, she was the hook. He could all but see the finished product unfolding.

Still, he wanted the big pull, something with punch and drama. This brought him right back to Clarissa. He needed that interview with Alice Van Camp, and another with someone who'd been directly involved in the Ridehour case. A.J. might try to block his way. He'd just have to roll over her.

How many times had he thought of her in the past three days? Too many. How often did he catch his mind drifting back to those few moments on the beach? Too often. And how much did he want to hold her like that again, close and hard? Too much.

Aurora. He knew it was dangerous to think of her as Aurora. Aurora was soft and accessible. Aurora was passionate and giving and just a little unsure of herself. He'd be smarter to remember A. J. Fields, tough, uncompromising and prickly around the edges. But it was late and his rooms were quiet. It was Aurora he thought of. It was Aurora he wanted.

On impulse, David picked up the phone. He punched buttons quickly, without giving himself a chance to think the action through. The phone rang four times before she answered.

"Fields."

"Good morning."

"David?" A.J. reached up to grab the towel before it slipped from her dripping hair.

"Yeah. How are you?"

"Wet." She switched the phone from hand to hand as she struggled into a robe. "I just stepped out of the shower. Is there a problem?"

The problem was, he mused, that he was three thousand miles away and was wondering what her skin would look like gleaming with water. He reached for another cigarette and found the pack empty. "No, should there be?"

"I don't usually get calls at this hour unless there is. When did you get back?"

"I didn't."

"You didn't? You mean you're still in New York?"

He stretched back in his chair and closed his eyes. Funny, he hadn't realized just how much he'd wanted to hear her voice. "Last time I looked."

"It's only ten your time. What are you doing up so early?"

"Haven't been to bed yet."

This time she wasn't quick enough to snatch the towel before it landed on her bare feet. A.J. ignored it as she dragged her fingers through the tangle of wet hair. "I see. The night life in Manhattan's very demanding, isn't it?"

He opened his eyes to glance at his piles of papers, overflowing ashtrays and empty coffee cups. "Yeah, it's all dancing till dawn."

"I'm sure." Scowling, she bent down to pick up her towel. "Well, you must have something important on your mind to break off the partying and call. What is it?"

"I wanted to talk to you."

"So I gathered." She began, more roughly than necessary, to rub the towel over her hair. "About what?"

"Nothing."

"Brady, have you been drinking?"

He gave a quick laugh as he settled back again. He couldn't even remember the last time he'd eaten. "No. Don't you believe in friendly conversations, A.J.?"

"Sure, but not between agents and producers long-distance at dawn."

"Try something new," he suggested. "How are you?"

Cautious, she sat on the bed. "I'm fine. How are you?"

"That's good. That's a very good start." With a yawn, he realized he could sleep in the chair without any trouble at all. "I'm a little tired, actually. We spent most of the day interviewing parapsychologists who use computers and mathematical equations. I talked to a woman who claims to have had a half a dozen out of body experiences. 'OOBs.'"

She couldn't prevent the smile. "Yes, I've heard the term."

"Claimed she traveled to Europe that way."

"Saves on airfare."

"I suppose."

She felt a little tug of sympathy, a small glimmer of amusement. "Having trouble separating the wheat from the chaff, Brady?"

"You could call it that. In any case, it looks like we're going to be running around on the East Coast awhile. A palmist in the mountains of western Maryland, a house in

Virginia that's supposed to be haunted by a young girl and a cat. There's a hypnotist in Pennsylvania who specializes in regression."

"Fascinating. It sounds like you're having just barrels of fun."

"I don't suppose you have any business that would bring you out this way."

"No, why?"

"Let's just say I wouldn't mind seeing you."

She tried to ignore the fact that the idea pleased her. "David, when you put things like that I get weak in the knees."

"I'm not much on the poetic turn of phrase." He wasn't handling this exactly as planned, he thought with a scowl. Then again, he hadn't given himself time to plan. Always a mistake. "Look, if I said I'd been thinking about you, that I wanted to see you, you'd just say something nasty. I'd end up paying for an argument instead of a conversation."

"And you can't afford to go over budget."

"See?" Still, it amused him. "Let's try a little experiment here. I've been watching experiments for days and I think I've got it down."

A.J. lay back on the bed. The fact that she was already ten minutes behind schedule didn't occur to her. "What sort of experiment?"

"You say something nice to me. Now that'll be completely out of character, so we'll start with that premise. . . . Go ahead," he prompted after fifteen seconds of blank silence.

"I'm trying to think of something."

"Don't be cute, A.J."

"All right, here. Your documentary on women in government was very informative and completely unbiased. I felt it showed a surprising lack of male, or female, chauvinism."

"That's a start, but why don't you try something a little more personal?"

"More personal," she mused, and smiled at the ceiling. When had she last lain on her bed and flirted over the phone? Had she ever? She supposed it didn't hurt, with a distance of three thousand miles, to feel sixteen and giddy. "How about this? If you ever decide you want to try the other end of the camera, I can make you a star."

"Too clichéd," David decided, but found himself grinning.

"You're very picky. How about if I said I think you might, just might, make an interesting companion. You're not difficult to look at, and your mind isn't really dull."

"Very lukewarm, A.J."

"Take it or leave it."

"Why don't we take the experiment to the next stage? Spend an evening with me and find out if your hypothesis is correct."

"I'm afraid I can't dump everything here and fly out to Pennsylvania or wherever to test a theory."

"I'll be back the middle of next week."

She hesitated, lectured herself, then went with impulse. "*Double Bluff* is opening here next week. Friday. Hastings Reed is a client. He's certain he's going to cop the Oscar."

"Back to business, A.J.?"

"I happen to have two tickets for the premiere. You buy the popcorn."

She'd surprised him. Switching the phone to his other hand, David was careful to speak casually. "A date?"

"Don't push your luck, Brady."

"I'll pick you up on Friday."

"Eight," she told him, already wondering if she was making a mistake. "Now go to bed. I have to get to work."

"Aurora."

"Yes?"

"Give me a thought now and then."

"Good night, Brady."

A.J. hung up the phone, then sat with it cradled in her lap. What had possessed her to do that? She'd intended to give the tickets away and catch the film when the buzz had died down. She didn't care for glittery premieres in the first place. And more important, she knew spending an evening with David Brady was foolish. And dangerous.

When was the last time she'd allowed herself to be charmed by a man? A million years ago, she remembered with a sigh. And where had that gotten her? Weepy and disgusted with herself. But she wasn't a child anymore, she remembered. She was a successful, self-confident woman who could handle ten David Bradys at a negotiating table. The problem was she just wasn't sure she could handle one of him anywhere else.

She let out a long lingering sigh before her gaze passed over her clock. With a muffled oath she was tumbling out of bed. Damn David Brady and her own foolishness. She was going to be late.

Chapter Five

She bought a new dress. A.J. told herself that as the agent representing the lead in a major motion picture premiering in Hollywood, she was obligated to buy one. But she knew she had bought it for Aurora, not A.J.

At five minutes to eight on Friday night, she stood in front of her mirror and studied the results. No chic, professional suit this time. But perhaps she shouldn't have gone so far in the other direction.

Still, it was black. Black was practical and always in vogue. She turned to the right profile, then the left. It certainly wasn't flashy. But all in all, it might have been wiser to have chosen something more conservative than the pipeline strapless, nearly backless black silk. Straight on, it was provocative. From the side it was downright suggestive. Why hadn't she noticed in the dressing room just how tightly the material clung? Maybe she had, A.J. admitted on a long breath. Maybe she'd been giddy enough, foolish enough, to buy it because it didn't make her feel like an agent or any other sort of professional. It just made her feel like a woman. That was asking for trouble.

In any case, she could solve part of the problem with the little beaded jacket. Satisfied, she reached for a heavy silver locket clipped to thick links. Even as she was fastening it, A.J. heard the door. Taking her time, she slipped into the shoes that lay neatly at the foot of her bed, checked the contents of her purse and picked up the beaded jacket. Reminding herself to think of the entire process as an experiment, she opened the door to David.

She hadn't expected him to bring her flowers. He didn't seem the type for such time-honored romantic gestures. Because he appeared to be as off-balance as she, they just stood there a moment, staring.

She was stunning. He'd never considered her beautiful before. Attractive, yes, and sexy in the coolest, most aloof sort of way. But tonight she was breathtaking. Her dress didn't glitter, it didn't gleam, but simply flowed with the long, subtle lines of her body. It was enough. More than enough.

He took a step forward. Clearing her throat, A.J. took a step back.

"Right on time," she commented, and worked on a smile.

"I'm already regretting I didn't come early."

A.J. accepted the roses and struggled to be casual, when she wanted to bury her face in them. "Thank you. They're lovely. Would you like a drink while I put them in water?"

"No." It was enough just to look at her.

"I'll just be a minute."

As she walked away, his gaze passed down her nape over her shoulder blades and the smooth, generously exposed back to her waist, where the material of her dress again intruded. It nearly made him change his mind about the drink.

To keep his mind off tall blondes with smooth skin, he took a look around her apartment. She didn't appear to have the same taste in decorating as Clarissa.

The room was cool, as cool as its tenant, and just as streamlined. He couldn't fault the icy colors or the uncluttered lines, but he wondered just how much of herself Aurora Fields had put into the place she lived. In the manner of her office, nothing was out of place. No frivolous mementos were set out for public viewing. The room had class and style, but none of the passion he'd found in the woman.

And it told no secrets, not even in a whisper. He found himself more determined than ever to discover how many she had.

When A.J. came back she was steady. She'd arranged the roses in one of her rare extravagances, a tall, slim vase of Baccarat crystal. "Since you're prompt, we can get there a bit early and ogle the celebrities. It's different than dealing with them over a business lunch or watching a shoot."

"You look like a witch," he murmured. "White skin, black dress. You can almost smell the brimstone."

Her hands were no longer steady as she reached for her jacket. "I had an ancestor who was burned as one."

He took the jacket from her, regretting the fact that once it was on too much of her would be covered. "I guess I shouldn't be surprised."

"In Salem, during the madness." A.J. tried to ignore the way his fingers lingered as he slid the jacket over her. "Of course she was no more witch than Clarissa, but she was...special. According to the journals and documents that Clarissa gathered, she was twenty-five and very lovely. She made the mistake of warning her neighbors about a barn fire that didn't happen for two days."

"So she was tried and executed?"

"People usually have violent reactions to what they don't understand."

"We talked to a man in New York who's making a killing in the stock market by 'seeing' things before they happen."

"Times change." A.J. picked up her bag, then paused at the door. "My ancestor died alone and penniless. Her name was Aurora." She lifted a brow when he said nothing. "Shall we go?"

David slipped his hand over hers as the door shut at their backs. "I have a feeling that having an ancestor executed as a witch is very significant for you."

After shrugging, A.J. drew her hand from his to push the button for the elevator. "Not everyone has one in his family tree."

"And?"

"And let's just say I have a good working knowledge of how different opinions can be. They range from everything from blind condemnation to blind faith. Both extremes are dangerous."

As they stepped into the elevator he said consideringly, "And you work very hard to shield Clarissa from both ends."

"Exactly."

"What about you? Are you defending yourself by keeping your relationship with Clarissa quiet?"

"I don't need defending from my mother." She'd swung through the doors before she managed to bank the quick surge of temper. "It's easier for me to work for her if we keep the family relationship out of it."

"Logical. I find you consistently logical, A.J."

She wasn't entirely sure it was a compliment. "And there is the fact that I'm very accessible. I didn't want clients rushing in to ask me to have my mother tell them where they lost their diamond ring. Is your car in the lot?"

"No, we're right out front. And I wasn't criticizing, Aurora, just asking."

She felt the temper fade as quickly as it had risen. "It's all right. I tend to be a little sensitive where Clarissa's concerned. I don't see a car," she began, glancing idly past a gray limo before coming back to it with raised brows. "Well," she murmured. "I'm impressed."

"Good." The driver was already opening the door. "That was the idea."

A.J. snuggled in. She'd ridden in limos countless times, escorting clients, delivering or picking them up at airports.

But she never took such cushy comfort for granted. As she let herself enjoy, she watched David take a bottle out of ice.

"Flowers, a limo and now champagne. I am impressed, Brady, but I'm also—"

"Going to spoil it," he finished as he eased the cork expertly out. "Remember, we're testing your theory that I'd make an interesting companion." He offered a glass. "How'm I doing?"

"Fine so far." She sipped and appreciated. If she'd had experience in anything, she reminded herself, it was in how to keep a relationship light and undemanding. "I'm afraid I'm more used to doing the pampering than being pampered."

"How's it feel to be on the other side?"

"A little too good." She slipped out of her shoes and let her feet sink into the carpet. "I could just sit and ride for hours."

"It's okay with me." He ran a finger down the side of her throat to the edge of her jacket. "Want to skip the movie?"

She felt the tremor start where his finger skimmed, then rush all the way to the pit of her stomach. It came home to her that she hadn't had experience with David Brady. "I think not." Draining her glass, she held it out for a refill. "I suppose you attend a lot of these."

"Premieres?" He tilted wine in her glass until it fizzed to the rim. "No. Too Hollywood."

"Oh." With a gleam in her eye, A.J. glanced slowly around the limo. "I see."

"Tonight seemed to be an exception." He toasted her, appreciating the way she sat with such careless elegance in the plush corner of the limo. She belonged there. Now. With him. "As a representative of some of the top names in the business, you must drop in on these things a few times a year."

"No." A.J.'s lips curved as she sipped from her glass. "I hate them."

"Are you serious?"

"Deadly."

"Then what the hell are we doing?"

"Experimenting," she reminded him, and set her glass down as the limo stopped at the curb. "Just experimenting."

There were throngs of people crowded into the roped off sections by the theater's entrance. Cameras were clicking, flashes popping. It didn't seem to matter to the crowd that the couple alighting from the limo weren't recognizable faces. It was Hollywood. It was opening night. The glitz was peaking. A.J. and David were cheered and applauded. She blinked twice as three paparazzi held cameras in her face.

"Incredible, isn't it?" he muttered as he steered her toward the entrance.

"It reminds me why I agent instead of perform." In an instinctive defense she wasn't even aware of, she turned away from the cameras. "Let's find a dark corner."

"I'm for that."

She had to laugh. "You never give up."

"A.J. A.J., *darling*!"

Before she could react, she found herself crushed against a soft, generous bosom. "Merinda, how nice to see you."

"Oh, I can't tell you how thrilled I am you're here." Merinda MacBride, Hollywood's current darling, drew her dramatically away. "A friendly face, you know. These things are such zoos."

She glittered from head to foot, from the diamonds that hung at her ears to the sequined dress that appeared to have been painted on by a very appreciative artist. She sent A.J. a smile that would have melted chocolate at ten paces. "You look divine."

"Thank you. You aren't alone?"

"Oh, no. I'm with Brad...." After a moment's hesitation, she smiled again. "Brad," she repeated, as if she'd decided last names weren't important. "He's fetching me a drink." Her gaze shifted and fastened on David. "You're not alone, either."

"Merinda MacBride, David Brady."

"A pleasure." He took her hand and, though she turned her knuckles up expectantly, didn't bring it to his lips. "I've seen your work and admired it."

"Why, thank you." She studied, measured and rated him in a matter of seconds. "Are we mutual clients of A.J.'s?"

"David's a producer." A.J. watched Merinda's baby-blue eyes sharpen. "Of documentaries," she added, amused. "You might have seen some of his work on public television."

"Of course." She beamed at him, though she'd never watched public television in her life and had no intention of starting. "I desperately admire producers. Especially attractive ones."

"I have a couple of scripts I think you'd be interested in," A.J. put in to draw her off.

"Oh?" Instantly Merinda dropped the sex bomb act. A. J. Fields didn't recommend a script unless it had meat on it. "Have them sent over."

"First thing Monday."

"Well, I must find Brad before he forgets about me. David." She gave him her patented smoldering look. Documentaries or not, he was a producer. And a very attractive one. "I hope we run into each other again. Ta, A.J." She brushed cheeks. "Let's do lunch."

"Soon."

David barely waited for her to walk out of earshot. "You deal with that all the time?"

"Ssh!"

"I mean *all* the time," he continued, watching as Merinda's tightly covered hips swished through the crowd. "Day after day. Why aren't you crazy?"

"Merinda may be a bit overdramatic, but if you've seen any of her films, you'll know just how talented she is."

"The woman looked loaded with talent to me," he began, but stopped to grin when A.J. scowled. "As an *actress*," he continued. "I thought she was exceptional in *Only One Day*."

A.J. couldn't quite conquer the smile. She'd hustled for weeks to land Merinda that part. "So you have seen her films."

"I don't live in a cave. That film was the first one that didn't—let's say, focus on her anatomy."

"It was the first one I represented her on."

"She's fortunate in her choice of agents."

"Thank you, but it goes both ways. Merinda's a very hot property."

"If we're going to make it through this evening, I'd better not touch that one."

They were interrupted another half a dozen times before they could get into the theater. A.J. ran into clients, acquaintances and associates, greeted, kissed and complimented while turning down invitations to after-theater parties.

"You're very good at this." David took two seats on the aisle near the back of the theater.

"Part of the job." A.J. settled back. There was nothing she enjoyed quite so much as a night at the movies.

"A bit jaded, A.J.?"

"Jaded?"

"Untouched by the glamour of it all, unaffected by the star system. You don't get any particular thrill out of exchanging kisses and hugs with some of the biggest and most distinguished names in the business."

"Business," she repeated, as if that explained it all. "That's not being jaded—it's being sensible. And the only time I saw you awestruck was when you found yourself face to face with three inches of cleavage on a six-foot blonde. Ssh," she muttered before he could comment. "It's started and I hate to miss the opening credits."

With the theater dark, the audience quiet, A.J. threw herself into the picture. Ever since childhood, she'd been able to transport herself with the big screen. She wouldn't have called it "escape." She didn't like the word. A.J. called it "involvement." The actor playing the lead was a client, a man she knew intimately and had comforted through two divorces. All three of his children's birthdays were noted in her book. She'd listened to him rant; she'd heard his complaints, his doubts. That was all part of the job. But the moment she saw him on film, he was, to her, the part he played and nothing else.

Within five minutes, she was no longer in a crowded theater in Los Angeles, but in a rambling house in Connecticut. And there was murder afoot. When the lights went out and thunder boomed, she grabbed David's arm and cringed in her seat. Not one to pass up an age-old opportunity, he slipped an arm around her.

When was the last time, he wondered, that he'd sat in a theater with his arm around his date? He decided it had been close to twenty years and he'd been missing a great deal. He turned his attention to the film, but was distracted by her scent. It was still light, barely discernible, but it filled his senses. He tried to concentrate on the action and drama racing across the screen. A.J. caught her breath and shifted an inch closer. The tension on the screen seemed very pedestrian compared to his own. When the lights came up he found himself regretting that there was no longer such a thing as the double feature.

"It was good, wasn't it?" Eyes brilliant with pleasure, she turned to him. "It was really very good."

"Very good," he agreed, and lifted his hand to toy with her ear. "And if the applause is any indication, your client's got himself a hit."

"Thank God." She breathed a sigh of relief before shifting away to break what was becoming a very unnerving contact. "I talked him into the part. If he'd flopped, it would have been my head."

"And now that he can expect raves?"

"It'll be because of his talent," she said easily. "And that's fair enough. Would you mind if we slipped out before it gets too crazy?"

"I'd prefer it." He rose and steered her through the pockets of people that were already forming in the aisles. They hadn't gone ten feet before A.J.'s name was called out three times.

"Where are you going? You running out?" Hastings Reed, six feet three inches of down-home sex and manhood, blocked the aisle. He was flushed with the victory of seeing himself triumph on the screen and nervous that he might have misjudged the audience reaction. "You didn't like it?"

"It was wonderful." Understanding his need for reassurance, A.J. stood on tiptoe to brush his cheek. "You were wonderful. Never better."

He returned the compliment with a bone-crushing hug. "We have to wait for the reviews."

"Prepare to accept praise humbly, and with good grace. Hastings, this is David Brady."

"Brady?" As Hastings took David's hand, his etched in bronze face creased into a frown. "Producer?"

"That's right."

"God, I love your work." Already flying, Hastings pumped David's hand six times before finally releasing it.

"I'm an honorary chairman of the Rights for Abused Children. Your documentary did an incredible job of bringing the issue home and making people aware. Actually, it's what got me involved in the first place."

"It's good to hear that. We wanted to make people think."

"Made me think. I've got kids of my own. Listen, keep me in mind if you ever do a follow-up. No fee." He grinned down at A.J. "She didn't hear that."

"Hear what?"

He laughed and yanked her against him again. "This lady's incredible. I don't know what I'd have done without her. I wasn't going to take this part, but she badgered me into it."

"I never badger," A.J. said mildly.

"Nags, badgers and browbeats. Thank God." Grinning, he finally took a good look at her. "Damn if you don't look like something a man could swallow right up. I've never seen you dressed like that."

To cover a quick flush of embarrassment, she reached up to straighten his tie. "And as I recall, the last time I saw you, you were in jeans and smelled of horses."

"Guess I did. You're coming to Chasen's?"

"Actually, I—"

"You're coming. Look, I've got a couple of quick interviews, but I'll see you there in a half-hour." He took two strides away and was swallowed up in the crowd.

"He's got quite an . . . overwhelming personality," David commented.

"To say the least." A.J. glanced at her watch. It was still early. "I suppose I should at least put in an appearance, since he'll count on it now. I can take a cab if you'd rather skip it."

"Ever hear of the expression about leaving with the guy who brought you?"

"This isn't a country dance," A.J. pointed out as they wove through the lingering crowd.

"Same rules apply. I can handle Chasen's."

"Okay, but just for a little while."

The "little while" lasted until after three.

Cases of champagne, mountains of caviar and piles of fascinating little canapés. Even someone as practical as A.J. found it difficult to resist a full-scale celebration. The music was loud, but it didn't seem to matter. There were no quiet corners to escape to. Through her clientele and David's contacts, they knew nearly everyone in the room between them. A few minutes of conversation here, another moment there, ate up hours of time. Caught up in her client's success, A.J. didn't mind.

On the crowded dance floor, she allowed herself to relax in David's arms. "Incredible, isn't it?"

"Nothing tastes so sweet as success, especially when you mix it with champagne."

She glanced around. It was hard not to be fascinated with the faces, the names, the bodies. She was part of it, a very intricate part. But through her own choice, she wasn't an intimate part. "I usually avoid this sort of thing."

He let his fingers skim lightly up her back. "Why?"

"Oh, I don't know." Weariness, wine and pleasure combined. Her cheek rested against his. "I guess I'm more of a background sort of person. You fit in."

"And you don't?"

"Ummm." She shook her head. Why was it men smelled so wonderful—so wonderfully different? And felt so good when you held and were held by one. "You're part of the talent. I just work with clauses and figures."

"And that's the way you want it?"

"Absolutely. Still, this is nice." When his hand ran down her back again, she stretched into it. "Very nice."

"I'd rather be alone with you," he murmured. Every time he held her like this he thought he would go crazy. "In some dim little room where the music was low."

"This is safer." But she didn't object when his lips brushed her temple.

"Who needs safe?"

"I do. I need safe and ordered and sensible."

"Anyone who chooses to be involved in this business tosses safe, ordered and sensible out the window."

"Not me." She drew back to smile at him. It felt so good to relax, to flow with the evening, to let her steps match his without any conscious thought. "I just make the deals and leave the chances up to others."

"Take ten percent and run?"

"That's right."

"I might have believed that a few weeks ago. The problem is I've seen you with Clarissa."

"That's entirely different."

"True enough. I also saw you with Hastings tonight. You get wrapped up with your clients, A.J. You might be able to convince yourself they're just signatures, but I know better. You're a marshmallow."

Her brows drew together. "Ridiculous. Marshmallows get swallowed."

"They're also resilient. I admire that in you." He touched his lips to hers before she could move. "I'm beginning to realize I admire quite a bit in you."

She would have pulled away then, but he kept her close easily enough and continued to sway. "I don't mix business and personal feelings."

"You lie."

"I might play with the truth," she said, abruptly dignified, "but I don't lie."

"You were ready to turn handsprings tonight when that movie hit."

A.J. tossed her hair out of her face. He saw too much too easily. A man wasn't supposed to. "Have you any idea how I can use that as a lever? I'll get Hastings a million-five for his next movie."

"You'll 'get Hastings,'" David repeated. "Even your phrasing gives you away."

"You're picking up things that aren't there."

"No, I think I'm finding things you've squirreled away. Have you got a problem with the fact that I've decided I like you?"

Off-balance, she missed a step and found herself pressed even closer. "I think I'd handle it better if we still got on each other nerves."

"Believe me, you get on my nerves." Until his blood was on slow boil, his muscles knotting and stretching and the need racing. "There are a hundred people in this room and my mind keeps coming back to the fact that I could have you out of what there is of that dress in thirty seconds flat."

The chill arrowed down her back. "You know that's not what I meant. You'd be smarter to keep your mind on business."

"Smarter, safer. We're looking for different things, A.J."

"We can agree on that, anyway."

"We might agree on more if we gave ourselves the chance."

She didn't know exactly why she smiled. Perhaps it was because it sounded like a fantasy. She enjoyed watching them, listening to them without really believing in them. "David." She rested her arms on his shoulders. "You're a very nice man, on some levels."

"I think I can return that compliment."

"Let me spell things out for you in the way I understand best. Number one, we're business associates at the moment. This precludes any possibility that we could be seriously involved. Number two, while this documentary is being made my first concern is, and will continue to be, Clarissa's welfare. Number three, I'm very busy and what free time I have I use to relax in my own way—which is alone. And number four, I'm not equipped for relationships. I'm selfish, critical and disinterested."

"Very well put." He kissed her forehead in a friendly fashion. "Are you ready to go?"

"Yes." A little nonplussed by his reaction, she walked off the dance floor to retrieve her jacket. They left the noise and crowd behind and stepped out into the cool, early morning air. "I forget sometimes that the glamour and glitz can be nice in small doses."

He helped her into the waiting limo. "Moderation in all things."

"Life's more stable that way." Cut off from the driver and the outside by thick smoked glass, A.J. settled back against the seat. Before she could let out the first contented sigh, David was close, his hand firm on her chin. "David—"

"Number one," he began, "I'm the producer of this project, and you're the agent for one, only one, of the talents. That means we're business associates in the broadest sense and that doesn't preclude an involvement. We're already involved."

There'd been no heat in his eyes on the dance floor, she thought quickly. Not like there was now. "David—"

"You had your say," he reminded her. "Number two, while this documentary is being made, you can fuss over Clarissa all you want. That has nothing to do with us. Number three, we're both busy, which means we don't want to waste time with excuses and evasions that don't hold water. And number four, whether you think you're equipped for relationships or not, you're in the middle of one right now. You'd better get used to it."

Temper darkened her eyes and chilled her voice. "I don't have to get used to anything."

"The hell you don't. Put a number on this."

Frustrated desire, unrelieved passion, simmering anger. She felt them all as his mouth crushed down on hers. Her first reaction was pure self-preservation. She struggled against him, knowing if she didn't free herself quickly, she'd be lost. But he seemed to know, somehow, that her struggle was against herself, not him.

He held her closer. His mouth demanded more, until, despite fears, despite doubts, despite everything, she gave.

With a muffled moan, her arms went around him. Her fingers slid up his back to lose themselves in his hair. Passion, still unrelieved, mounted until it threatened to consume. She could feel everything, the hard line of his body against hers, the soft give of the seat at her back. There was the heat of his lips as they pressed and rubbed on hers and the cool air blown in silently through the vents.

And she could taste—the lingering punch of champagne as their tongues tangled together. She could taste a darker flavor, a deeper flavor that was his flesh. Still wilder, less recognizable, was the taste of her own passion.

His mouth left hers only to search out other delights. Over the bare, vulnerable skin of her neck and shoulders he found them. His hands weren't gentle as they moved over her. His mouth wasn't tender. Her heart began to thud in a fast, chaotic rhythm at the thought of being taken with such hunger, such fury.

Driven by her own demons she let her hands move, explore and linger. When his breath was as uneven as hers their lips met again. The contact did nothing to soothe and everything to arouse. Desperate for more, she brought her teeth down to nip, to torment. With an oath, he swung her around until they were sprawled on the long wide seat.

Her lips parted as she looked up at him. She could see the intermittent flash of streetlights as they passed overhead. Shadow and light. Shadow and light. Hypnotic. Erotic. A.J. reached up to touch his face.

She was all cream and silk as she lay beneath him. Her hair was tousled around a face flushed with arousal. The touch of her fingers on his cheek was light as a whisper and caused the need to thunder through him.

"This is crazy," she murmured.

"I know."

"It's not supposed to happen." But it was. She knew it. She had known it from the first meeting. "It can't happen," she corrected.

"Why?"

"Don't ask me." Her voice dropped to a whisper. She couldn't resist letting her fingers play along his face even as she prepared herself to deny both of them. "I can't explain. If I could you wouldn't understand."

"If there's someone else I don't give a damn."

"No, there's no one." She closed her eyes a moment, then opened them again to stare at him. "There's no one else."

Why was he hesitating? She was here, aroused, inches away from total surrender. He had only to ignore the confused plea in her eyes and take. But even with his blood hot, the need pressing, he couldn't ignore it. "It might not be now, it might not be here, but it will be, Aurora."

It would be. Had to be. The part of her that knew it fought a frantic tug-of-war with the part that had to deny it. "Let me go, David."

Trapped by his own feelings, churning with his own needs, he pulled her up. "What kind of game are you playing?"

She was cold. Freezing. She felt each separate chill run over her skin. "It's called survival."

"Damn it, Aurora." She was so beautiful. Why did she suddenly have to be so beautiful? Why did she suddenly have to look so fragile? "What does being with me, making love with me, have to do with your survival?"

"Nothing." She nearly laughed as she felt the limo cruise to a halt. "Nothing at all if it were just that simple."

"Why complicate it? We want each other. We're both adults. People become lovers every day without doing themselves any damage."

"Some people." She let out a shuddering breath. "I'm not some people. If it were so simple, I'd make love with you right here, in the back seat of this car. I won't tell you I don't want to." She turned to look at him and the vulnerability in her eyes was haunted by regrets. "But it's not simple. Making love with you would be easy. Falling in love with you wouldn't."

Before he could move, she'd pushed open the door and was on the street.

"Aurora." He was beside her, a hand on her arm, but she shook him off. "You can't expect to just walk off after a statement like that."

"That's just what I'm doing," she corrected, and shook him off a second time.

"I'll take you up." With what willpower he had left he held on to patience.

"No. Just go."

"We have to talk."

"No." Neither of them was prepared for the desperation in her voice. "I want you to go. It's late. I'm tired. I'm not thinking straight."

"If we don't talk this out now, we'll just have to do it later."

"Later, then." She would have promised him anything for freedom at that moment. "I want you to go now, David."

When he continued to hold her, her voice quivered. "Please, I need you to go. I can't handle this now."

He could fight her anger, but he couldn't fight her fragility. "All right."

He waited until she had disappeared inside her building. Then he leaned back on the car and pulled out a cigarette. Later then, he promised himself. They'd talk. He stood where he was, waiting for his system to level. They'd talk, he assured himself again. But it was best to wait until they were both calmer and more reasonable.

Tossing away the cigarette, he climbed back into the limo. He hoped to God he could stop thinking of her long enough to sleep.

Chapter Six

She wanted to pace. She wanted to walk up and down, pull at her hair and walk some more. She forced herself to sit quietly on the sofa and wait as Clarissa poured tea.

"I'm so glad you came by, dear. It's so seldom you're able to spend an afternoon with me."

"Things are under control at the office. Abe's covering for me."

"Such a nice man. How's his little grandson?"

"Spoiled rotten. Abe wants to buy him Dodger Stadium."

"Grandparents are entitled to spoil the way parents are obliged to discipline." She kept her eyes lowered, anxious not to show her own longings and apply pressure. "How's your tea?"

"It's...different." Knowing the lukewarm compliment would satisfy Clarissa saved her from an outright lie. "What is it?"

"Rose hips. I find it very soothing in the afternoons. You seem to need a little soothing, Aurora."

A.J. set down her cup and, giving in to the need for movement, rose. She'd known when she'd deliberately cleared her calendar that she would come to Clarissa. And she'd known that she would come for help, though she'd repeatedly told herself she didn't need it.

"Momma." A.J. sat on the sofa again as Clarissa sipped tea and waited patiently. "I think I'm in trouble."

"You ask too much of yourself." Clarissa reached out to touch her hand. "You always have."

"What am I going to do?"

Clarissa sat back as she studied her daughter. She'd never heard that phrase from her before, and now that she had, she wanted to be certain to give the right answers. "You're frightened."

"Terrified." She was up again, unable to sit. "It's getting away from me. I'm losing the controls."

"Aurora, it isn't always necessary to hold on to them."

"It is for me." She looked back with a half smile. "You should understand."

"I do. Of course I do." But she'd wished so often that her daughter, her only child, would be at peace with herself. "You constantly defend yourself against being hurt because you were hurt once and decided it would never happen again. Aurora, are you in love with David?"

Clarissa would know he was at the core of it. Naturally she would know without a word being said. A.J. could accept that. "I might be if I don't pull myself back now."

"Would it be so bad to love someone?"

"David isn't just someone. He's too strong, too overwhelming. Besides..." She paused long enough to steady herself. "I thought I was in love once before."

"You were young." Clarissa came as close as she ever did to true anger. She set her cup in its saucer with a little snap. "Infatuation is a different matter. It demands more and gives less back than love."

A.J. stood in the middle of the room. There was really no place to go. "Maybe this is just infatuation. Or lust."

Clarissa lifted a brow and sipped tea calmly. "You're the only one who can answer that. Somehow I don't think you'd have cleared your calendar and come to see me in the middle of a workday if you were concerned about lust."

Laughing, A.J. walked over to drop on the sofa beside her. "Oh, Momma, there's no one like you. No one."

"Things were never normal for you, were they?"

"No." A.J. dropped her head on Clarissa's shoulder. "They were better. You were better."

"Aurora, your father loved me very much. He loved, and he accepted, without actually understanding. I can't even comprehend what my life might have been like if I hadn't given up the controls and loved him back."

"He was special," A.J. murmured. "Most men aren't."

Clarissa hesitated only a moment, then cleared her throat. "Alex accepts me, too."

"Alex?" Uneasy, A.J. sat up again. There was no mistaking the blush of color in Clarissa's cheeks. "Are you and Alex..." How did one put such a question to a mother? "Are you serious about Alex?"

"He asked me to marry him."

"What?" Too stunned for reason, A.J. jerked back and gaped. "Marriage? You barely know him. You met only weeks ago. Momma, certainly you're mature enough to realize something as important as marriage takes a great deal of thought."

Clarissa beamed at her. "What an excellent mother you'll make one day. I was never able to lecture quite like that."

"I don't mean to lecture." Mumbling, A.J. picked up her tea. "I just don't want you to jump into something like this without giving it the proper thought."

"You see, that's just what I mean. I'm sure you got that from your father's side. My family's always been just the tiniest bit flighty."

"Momma—"

"Do you remember when Alex and I were discussing palm reading for the documentary?"

"Of course." The uneasiness increased, along with a sense of inevitability. "You felt something."

"It was very strong and very clear. I admit it flustered me a bit to realize a man could be attracted to me after all these years. And I wasn't aware until that moment that I could feel like that about anyone."

"But you need time. I don't doubt anything you feel, anything you see. You know that. But—"

"Darling, I'm fifty-six." Clarissa shook her head, wondering how it had happened so quickly. "I've been content to live alone. I think perhaps I was meant to live alone for a certain amount of time. Now I want to share the rest of life. You're twenty-eight and content and very capable of living alone. Still, you mustn't be afraid to share your life."

"It's different."

"No." She took A.J.'s hands again. "Love, affection, needs. They're really very much the same for everyone. If David is the right man for you, you'll know it. But after knowing, you have to accept."

"He may not accept me." Her fingers curled tightly around her mother's. "I have trouble accepting myself."

"And that's the only worry you've ever given me. Aurora, I can't tell you what to do. I can't look into tomorrow for you as much as part of me wants to."

"I'm not asking that. I'd never ask you that."

"No, you wouldn't. Look into your heart, Aurora. Stop calculating risks and just look."

"I might see something I don't want to."

"Oh, you probably will." With a little laugh, Clarissa settled back on the sofa with an arm around A.J. "I can't tell you what to do, but I can tell you what I feel. David Brady is a very good man. He has his flaws, of course, but he is a good man. It's been a pleasure for me to be able to work with him. As a matter of fact, when he called this morning, I was delighted."

"Called?" Immediately alert, A.J. sat up straight. "David called you? Why?"

"Oh, a few ideas he'd had about the documentary." She fussed with the little lace napkin in her lap. "He's in Rolling Hills today. Well, not exactly in, but outside. Do you remember hearing about that old mansion no one ever seems able to live in for long? The one a few miles off the beach?"

"It's supposed to be haunted," A.J. muttered.

"Of course there are differing opinions on that. I think David made an excellent choice for his project, though, from what he told me about the background."

"What do you have to do with that?"

"That? Oh, nothing at all. We just chatted about the house. I suppose he thought I'd be interested."

"Oh." Mollified, A.J. began to relax. "That's all right then."

"We did set up a few other things. I'll be going into the studio—Wednesday," she decided. "Yes, I'm sure it's Wednesday of next week to discuss spontaneous phenomena. And then, oh, sometime the following week, I'm to go to the Van Camps'. We'll tape in Alice's living room."

"The Van Camps'." She felt the heat rising. "He set all this up with you."

Clarissa folded her hands. "Yes, indeed. Did I do something wrong?"

"Not you." Fired up, she rose. "He knew better than to change things without clearing it with me first. You can't trust anyone. Especially a producer." Snatching up her purse, she strode to the door. "You don't go anywhere on Wednesday to discuss any kind of phenomena until I see just what he has up his sleeve." She caught herself and came back to give Clarissa a hug. "Don't worry, I'll straighten it out."

"I'm counting on it." Clarissa watched her daughter storm out of the house before she sat back, content. She'd done everything she could—set energy in motion. The rest was up to fate.

"Tell him we'll reschedule. Better yet, have Abe meet with him." A.J. shouted into her car phone as she came up behind a tractor-trailer.

"Abe has a three-thirty. I don't think he can squeeze Montgomery in at four."

"Damn." Impatient, A.J. zoomed around the tractor-trailer. "Who's free at four?"

"Just Barbara."

While keeping an eye peeled for her exit, A.J. turned that over in her mind. "No, they'd never jell. Reschedule, Diane. Tell Montgomery... tell him there was an emergency. A medical emergency."

"Check. There isn't, is there?"

Her smile was set and nothing to laugh about. "There might be."

"Sounds promising. How can I reach you?"

"You can't. Leave anything important on the machine. I'll call in and check."

"You got it. Hey, good luck."

"Thanks." Teeth gritted, A.J. replaced the receiver.

He wasn't going to get away with playing power games. A.J. knew all the rules to that one, and had made up plenty of her own. David Brady was in for it. A.J. reached for her map again. If she could ever find him.

When the first raindrop hit the windshield she started to swear. By the time she'd taken the wrong exit, made three wrong turns and found herself driving down a decrepit gravel road in a full-fledged spring storm, she was cursing fluently. Every one of them was aimed directly at David Brady's head.

One look at the house through driving rain and thunderclouds proved why he'd chosen so well. Braking viciously,

A.J. decided he'd arranged the storm for effect. When she swung out of the car and stepped in a puddle of mud that slopped over her ankles, it was the last straw.

He saw her through the front window. Surprise turned to annoyance quickly at the thought of another interruption on a day that had seen everything go wrong. He hadn't had a decent night's sleep in a week, his work was going to hell and he itched just looking at her. When he pulled open the front door, he was as ready as A.J. for an altercation.

"What the hell are you doing here?"

Her hair was plastered to her face; her suit was soaked. She'd just ruined half a pair of Italian shoes. "I want to talk to you, Brady."

"Fine. Call my office and set up an appointment. I'm working."

"I want to talk to you now!" Lifting a hand to his chest, she gave him a hefty shove back against the door. "Just where do you come off making arrangements with one of my clients without clearing it with me? If you want Clarissa in the studio next week, then you deal with me. Understand?"

He took her damp hand by the wrist and removed it from his shirt. "I have Clarissa under contract for the duration of filming. I don't have to clear anything with you."

"You'd better read it again, Brady. Dates and times are set up through her representative."

"Fine. I'll send you a schedule. Now if you'll excuse me—"

He pushed open the door, but she stepped in ahead of him. Two electricians inside the foyer fell silent and listened. "I'm not finished."

"I am. Get lost, Fields, before I have you tossed off the set."

"Watch your step, or my client might develop a chronic case of laryngitis."

"Don't threaten me, A.J." He gripped her lapels with both hands. "I've had about all I'm taking from you. You want to talk, fine. Your office or mine, tomorrow."

"Mr. Brady, we need you upstairs."

For a moment longer he held her. Her gaze was locked on his and the fury was fierce and very equal. He wanted, God, he wanted to drag her just a bit closer, wipe that maddening look off her face. He wanted to crush his mouth to hers until she couldn't speak, couldn't breathe, couldn't fight. He wanted, more than anything, to make her suffer the way he suffered. He released her so abruptly she took two stumbling steps back.

"Get lost," he ordered, and turned to mount the stairs.

It took her a minute to catch her breath. She hadn't known she could get this angry, hadn't allowed herself to become this angry in too many years to count. Emotions flared up inside her, blinding her to everything else. She dashed up the stairs behind him.

"Ms. Fields, nice to see you again." Alex stood on the top landing in front of a wall where the paint had peeled and cracked. He gave her an easy smile as he smoked his cigar and waited to be called back in front of the camera.

"And I want to talk to you, too," she snapped at him. Leaving him staring, she strode down the hall after David.

It was narrow and dark. There were cobwebs clinging to corners, but she didn't notice. In places there were squares of lighter paint where pictures had once hung. A.J. worked her way through technicians and walked into the room only steps behind David.

It hit her like a wall. No sooner had she drawn in the breath to shout at him again than she couldn't speak at all. She was freezing. The chill whipped through her and to the bone in the matter of a heartbeat.

The room was lit for the shoot, but she didn't see the cameras, the stands or the coils of cable. She saw wallpaper, pink roses on cream, and a four-poster draped in the same rose hue. There was a little mahogany stool beside the bed that was worn smooth in the center. She could smell the roses that stood fresh and a little damp in an exquisite crystal vase on a mahogany vanity that gleamed with beeswax and lemon. And she saw—much more. And she heard.

You betrayed me. You betrayed me with him, Jessica.

No! No, I swear it. Don't. For God's sake don't do this. I love you. I—

Lies! All lies. You won't tell any more.

There were screams. There was silence, a hundred times worse. A.J.'s purse hit the floor with a thud as she lifted her hands to her ears.

"A.J." David was shaking her, hands firm on her shoulders, as everyone else in the room stopped to stare. "What's wrong with you?"

She reached out to clutch his shirt. He could feel the iciness of her flesh right through the cotton. She looked at him, but her eyes didn't focus. "That poor girl," she murmured. "Oh, God, that poor girl."

"A.J." With an effort, he kept his voice calm. She was shuddering and pale, but the worst of it was her eyes, dark and glazed as they looked beyond him. She stared at the center of the room as if held in a trance. He took both of her hands in his. "A.J., what girl?"

"He killed her right here. There on the bed. He used his hands. She couldn't scream anymore because his hands were on her throat, squeezing. And then . . ."

"A.J." He took her chin and forced her to look at him. "There's no bed in here. There's nothing."

"It—" She struggled for air, then lifted both hands to her face. The nausea came, a too familiar sensation. "I have to get out of here." Breaking away, she pushed through the technicians crowded in the doorway and ran. She stumbled out into the rain and down the porch steps before David caught her.

"Where are you going?" he demanded. A flash of lightning highlighted them both as the rain poured down.

"I've got to…" She trailed off and looked around blindly. "I'm going back to town. I have to get back."

"I'll take you."

"No." Panicked, she struggled, only to find herself held firmly. "I have my car."

"You're not driving anywhere like this." Half leading, half dragging, he pulled her to his car. "Now stay here," he ordered, and slammed the door on her.

Unable to gather the strength to do otherwise, A.J. huddled on the seat and shivered. She needed only a minute. She promised herself she needed only a minute to pull herself together. But however many it took David to come back, the shivering hadn't stopped. He tossed her purse in the back, then tucked a blanket around her. "One of the crew's taking your car back to town." After starting the engine, he headed down the bumpy, potholed gravel road. For several moments there was silence as the rain drummed and she sat hunched under the blanket.

"Why didn't you tell me?" he said at length.

She was better now. She took a steady breath to prove she had control. "Tell you what?"

"That you were like your mother."

A.J. curled into a ball on the seat, cradled her head in her arms and wept.

What the hell was he supposed to say? David cursed her, then himself, as he drove through the rain with her sobbing beside him. She'd given him the scare of his life when he'd turned around and had seen her standing there, gasping for air and white as a sheet. He'd never felt anything as cold as her hands had been. Never seen anything like what she must have seen.

Whatever doubts he had, whatever criticisms he could make about laboratory tests, five-dollar psychics and executive clairvoyants, he knew A.J. had seen something, felt something, none of the rest of them had.

So what did he do about it? What did he say?

She wept. She let herself empty. There was no use berating herself, no use being angry with what had happened. She'd long ago resigned herself to the fact that every now and again, no matter how careful she was, no matter how tightly controlled, she would slip and leave herself open.

The rain stopped. There was milky sunlight now. A.J. kept the blanket close around her as she straightened in her seat. "I'm sorry."

"I don't want an apology. I want an explanation."

"I don't have one." She wiped her cheeks dry with her hand. "I'd appreciate it if you'd take me home."

"We're going to talk, and we're going to do it where you can't kick me out."

She was too weak to argue, too weak to care. A.J. rested her head against the window and didn't protest when they passed the turn for her apartment. They drove up into the hills, high above the city. The rain had left things fresh here, though a curling mist still hugged the ground.

He turned into a drive next to a house with cedar shakes and tall windows. The lawn was wide and trimmed with spring flowers bursting around the borders.

"I thought you'd have a place in town."

"I used to, then I decided I had to breathe." He took her purse and a briefcase from the back seat. A.J. pushed the blanket aside and stepped from the car. Saying nothing, they walked to the front door together.

Inside wasn't rustic. He had paintings on the walls and thick Turkish carpets on the floors. She ran her hand along a polished rail and stepped down a short flight of steps into the living room. Still silent, David went to the fireplace and set kindling to blaze. "You'll want to get out of those wet clothes," he said matter-of-factly. "There's a bath upstairs at the end of the hall. I keep a robe on the back of the door."

"Thank you." Her confidence was gone—that edge that helped her keep one step ahead. A.J. moistened her lips. "David, you don't have to—"

"I'll make coffee." He walked through a doorway and left her alone.

She stood there while the flames from the kindling began to lick at split oak. The scent was woodsy, comfortable. She'd never felt more miserable in her life. The kind of rejection she felt now, from David, was the kind she'd expected. It was the kind she'd dealt with before.

She stood there while she battled back the need to weep again. She was strong, self-reliant. She wasn't about to break her heart over David Brady, or any man. Lifting her chin, A.J. walked to the stairs and up. She'd shower, let her clothes dry, then dress and go home. A. J. Fields knew how to take care of herself.

The water helped. It soothed her puffy eyes and warmed her clammy skin. From the small bag of emergency cosmetics in her purse, she managed to repair the worst of the damage. She tried not to notice that the robe carried David's scent as she slipped it on. It was better to remember that it was warm and covered her adequately.

When she went back downstairs, the living area was still empty. Clinging to the courage she'd managed to build back up, A.J. went to look for him.

The hallway twisted and turned at angles when least expected. If the situation had been different, A.J. would have appreciated the house for its uniqueness. She didn't take much notice of polished paneling offset by stark white walls, or planked floors scattered with intricately patterned carpets. She followed the hallway into the kitchen. The scent of coffee eased the beginning of flutters in her stomach. She took a moment to brace herself, then walked into the light.

He was standing by the window. There was a cup of coffee in his hand, but he wasn't drinking. Something was simmering on the stove. Perhaps he'd forgotten it. A.J. crossed her arms over her chest and rubbed her hands over the sleeves of the robe. She didn't feel warm any longer.

"David?"

He turned the moment she said his name, but slowly. He wasn't certain what he should say to her, what he could say. She looked so frail. He couldn't have described his own feelings at the moment and hadn't a clue to hers. "The coffee's hot," he told her. "Why don't you sit down?"

"Thanks." She willed herself to behave as normally as he and took a seat on a stool at the breakfast bar.

"I thought you could use some food." He walked to the stove to pour coffee. "I heated up some soup."

Tension began to beat behind her eyes. "You didn't have to bother."

Saying nothing, he ladled out the soup, then brought both it and the coffee to her. "It's an old family recipe. My mother always says a bowl of soup cures anything."

"It looks wonderful," she managed, and wondered why she had to fight back the urge to cry again. "David..."

"Eat first." Taking no food for himself, he drew up a stool across from her and cradled his coffee. He lit a cigarette and sat, sipping his coffee and smoking, while she toyed with her soup. "You're supposed to eat it," he pointed out. "Not just rearrange the noodles."

"Why don't you ask?" she blurted out. "I'd rather you just asked and got it over with."

So much hurt there, he realized. So much pain. He wondered where it had its roots. "I don't intend to start an interrogation, A.J."

"Why not?" When she lifted her head, her face was defiant, her eyes strong. "You want to know what happened to me in that room."

He blew out a stream of smoke before he crushed out his cigarette. "Of course I do. But I don't think you're ready to talk about what happened in that room. At least not in detail. A.J., why don't you just talk to me?"

"Not ready?" She might have laughed if her stomach wasn't tied up in knots. "You're never ready. I can tell you what she looked like—black hair, blue eyes. She was wearing a cotton gown that buttoned all the way up to her throat, and her name was Jessica. She was barely eighteen when her husband killed her in a jealous rage, strangled her with his own hands, then killed himself in grief with the pistol in the table beside the bed. That's what you want for your documentary, isn't it?"

The details, and the cool, steady way she delivered them, left him shaken. Just who was this woman who sat across from him, this woman he'd held and desired? "What happened to you has nothing to do with the project. I think it has a great deal to do with the way you're reacting now."

"I can usually control it." She shoved the soup aside so that it lapped over the edges of the bowl. "God knows I've had years of practice. If I hadn't been so angry, so out of control when I walked in there—it probably wouldn't have happened."

"You can block it."

"Usually, yes. To a large extent, anyway."

"Why do you?"

"Do you really think this is a gift?" she demanded as she pushed away from the counter. "Oh, maybe for someone like Clarissa it is. She's so unselfish, so basically good and content with herself."

"And you?"

"I hate it." Unable to remain still, she whirled away. "You've no idea what it can be like, having people stare at you, whisper. If you're different, you're a freak, and I—" She broke off, rubbing at her temple. When she spoke again, her voice was quiet. "I just wanted to be normal. When I was little, I'd have dreams." She folded her hands together and pressed them to her lips. "They were so incredibly real, but I was just a child and thought everyone dreamed like that. I'd tell one of my friends—oh, your cat's going to have kittens. Can I have the little white one? Then weeks later, the cat would have kittens and one of them would be white. Little things. Someone would lose a doll or a toy and I'd say, well, your mother put it on the top shelf in your closet. She forgot. When they looked it would be there. Kids didn't think much of it, but it made some of the parents nervous. They thought it would be best if their children stayed away from me."

"And that hurt," he murmured.

"Yes, that hurt a lot. Clarissa understood. She was comforting and really wonderful about it, but it hurt. I still had the dreams, but I stopped talking about them. Then my father died."

She stood, the heels of her hands pressed to her eyes as she struggled to rein in her emotions. "No, please." She shook her head as she heard David shift on the stool as if to rise. "Just give me a minute." On a long breath, she dropped her hands. "I knew he was dead. He was away on a selling trip, and I woke up in the middle of the night and knew. I got up and went into Clarissa. She was sitting up in bed, wide-awake. I could see on her face that she was already grieving. We didn't even say anything to each other, but I got into bed with her, and we just lay there together until the phone rang."

"And you were eight," he murmured, trying to get some grip on it.

"I was eight. After that, I started to block it off. Whenever I began to feel something, I'd just pull in. It got to the point where I could go for months—at one point, two years—without something touching it off. If I get angry or upset to the point where I lose control, I open myself up for it."

He remembered the way she'd stormed into the house, strong and ready for a fight. And the way she'd run out again, pale and terrified. "And I make you angry."

She turned to look at him for the first time since she'd begun to speak. "It seems that way."

The guilt was there. David wasn't certain how to deal with it, or his own confusion. "Should I apologize?"

"You can't help being what you are any more than I can stop being what I am."

"Aurora, I think I understand your need to keep a handle on this thing, not to let it interfere with the day-to-day. I don't understand why you feel you have to lock it out of your life like a disease."

She'd gone this far, she thought as she walked back to the counter. She'd finish. "When I was twenty, scrambling around and trying to get my business rolling, I met this man. He had this little shop on the beach, renting surfboards, selling lotion, that sort of thing. It was so, well, exciting, to see someone that free-spirited, that easygoing, when I was working ten hours a day just to scrape by. In any case, I'd never been involved seriously with a man before. There hadn't been time. I fell flat on my face for this one. He was fun, not too demanding. Before I knew it we were on the point of being engaged. He bought me this little ring with the promise of diamonds and emeralds once we hit it big. I think he meant it." She gave a little laugh as she slid onto the stool again. "In any case, I felt that if we were going to be married we shouldn't have any secrets."

"You hadn't told him?"

"No." She said it defiantly, as if waiting for disapproval. When none came, she lowered her gaze and went on. "I introduced him to Clarissa, and then I told him that I—I told him," she said flatly. "He thought it was a joke, sort of dared me to prove it. Because I felt so strongly about having everything up front between us, well, I guess you could say I proved it. After—he looked at me as though..." She swallowed and struggled to keep the hurt buried.

"I'm sorry."

"I suppose I should have expected it." Though she shrugged it off, she picked up the spoon and began to run the handle through her fingers. "I didn't see him for days after that. I went to him with some grand gesture in mind like giving him back his ring. It's almost funny, looking back on it now, the way he wouldn't look at me, the way he kept his distance. Too weird." She looked up again with a brittle smile. "I was just plain too weird."

And she was still hurting. But he didn't reach out to her. He wasn't quite sure how. "The wrong man at the wrong time."

A.J. gave an impatient shake of her head. "I was the wrong woman. Since then, I've learned that honesty isn't always the most advantageous route. Do you have any idea what it would do to me professionally if my clients knew? Those I didn't lose would ask me to tell them what role to audition for. People would start asking me to fly to Vegas with them so I could tell them what number to bet at the roulette table."

"So you and Clarissa downplay your relationship and you block the rest off."

"That's right." She picked up her cold coffee and downed it. "After today, I guess that goes to hell."

"I told Sam I'd discussed what had happened in that room with you, that we'd talked about the murder and coming up there had upset you." He rose to fetch the pot and freshen her coffee. "The crew may mumble about overimaginative women, but that's all."

She shut her eyes. She hadn't expected sensitivity from him, much less understanding. "Thanks."

"It's your secret if you feel it's necessary to keep it, A.J."

"It's very necessary. How did you feel when you realized?" she demanded. "Uncomfortable? Uneasy? Even now, you're tiptoeing around me."

"Maybe I am." He started to pull out a cigarette, then shoved it back into the pack. "Yeah, it makes me uneasy. It's not something I've ever had to deal with before. A man has to wonder if he'll have any secrets from a woman who can look inside him."

"Of course." She rose, back straight. "And a man's entitled to protect himself. I appreciate what you've done, David. I'm sure my clothes are dry now. I'll change if you'll call me a cab."

"No." He was up and blocking her way before she could walk out of the kitchen.

"Don't make this any more difficult for me, or for yourself."

"Damned if I want to," he muttered, and found he'd already reached for her. "I can't seem to help it. You make me uneasy," he repeated. "You've made me uneasy all along. I still want you, Aurora. That's all that seems to matter at the moment."

"You'll think differently later."

He drew her closer. "Reading my mind?"

"Don't joke."

"Maybe it's time someone did. If you want to look into my head now, you'll see that all I can think about is taking you upstairs, to my bed."

Her heart began to beat, in her chest, in her throat. "And tomorrow?"

"The hell with tomorrow." He brought his lips down to hers with a violence that left her shaken. "The hell with everything but the fact that you and I have a need for each other. You're not going home tonight, Aurora."

She let herself go, let herself risk. "No, I'm not."

Chapter Seven

There was moonlight, streaks of it, glimmering. She could smell the hyacinths, light and sweet, through the open windows. The murmur of a stream winding its way through the woods beside the house was quiet, soothing. Every muscle in A.J.'s body tensed as she stepped into David's bedroom.

The painting hung on the wall as she knew it would, vivid, sensual streaks on a white canvas. The first shudder rolled through her as she turned her head and saw her own vague reflection, not in a mirror, but in a tall glass door.

"I dreamed this." The words were barely audible as she took a step back. But was she stepping back into the dream or into reality? Were they somehow both the same? Panicked, she stood where she was. Didn't she have a choice? she asked herself. Was she just following a pattern already set, a pattern that had begun the moment David Brady had walked into her office?

"This isn't what I want," she whispered, and turned—for escape, for freedom—in denial, she couldn't have said. But he was there, blocking her way, drawing her closer, drawing her in just as she'd known he would be.

She looked up at him as she knew she had done before. His face was in shadows, as indistinct as hers had been in the glass. But his eyes were clear, highlighted by moonlight. His words were clear, highlighted by desire.

"You can't keep running, Aurora, not from yourself, not from me."

There was impatience in his voice, impatience that became all the sharper when his mouth closed over hers. He wanted, more desperately than he had allowed himself to believe. He needed, more intensely than he could afford to admit. Her uncertainty, her hesitation, aroused some deep, primitive part of him. Demand, take, possess. The thoughts twined together into one throbbing pulsebeat of desire. He didn't feel the pleasant anticipation he had with other women, but a rage, burning, almost violent. As he tasted the first hint of surrender, he nearly went mad with it.

His mouth was so hungry, his hands so strong. The pressure of his body against hers was insistent. He held her as though she were his to take with or without consent. Yet she knew, had always known, the choice was ultimately hers. She could give or deny. Like a stone tossed into clear water, her decision now would send ripples flowing out into her life. Where they ended, how they altered the flow, couldn't be foretold. To give, she knew, was always a risk. And risk always held its own excitement, its own fear. With each second that passed, the pleasure grew more bold and ripe, until with a moan of acceptance, she brought her hands to his face and let herself go.

It was only passion, A.J. told herself while her body strained and ached. Passion followed no patterns, kept to no course. The need that grew inside her had nothing to do with dreams or hopes or wishes. It was her passion she couldn't resist, his passion she couldn't refuse. For tonight, this one night, she'd let herself be guided by it.

He knew the instant she was his. Her body didn't weaken, but strengthened. The surrender he'd expected became a hunger as urgent as his. There would be no slow seduction for either of them, no gentle persuasion. Desire was a razor's edge that promised as much pain as pleasure. They both understood it; they both acknowledged; they both accepted. Together they fell onto the bed and let the fire blaze.

His robe tangled around her. With an impatient oath, he yanked it down from her shoulder so that the tantalizing slope was exposed. His lips raced over her face, leaving hers unfulfilled while he stoked a line of heat down her throat. She felt the rasp of his cheek and moaned in approval. He sought to torment, he sought to dominate, but she met each move with equal strength. She felt the warm trace of his tongue and shivered in anticipation. Unwilling to leave the reins in his hands, she tugged at the buttons of his shirt, unfastening, tearing, until with her own patience ended, she ripped it from his back.

His flesh was taut under her palms, the muscles a tight ridge to be explored and exploited. Male, hard, strong. His scent wound its way into her senses, promising rough demands and frantic movement. She tasted furious demands, hot intentions, then her excitement bounded upward when she felt his first tremble. Painful, urgent, desperate needs poured from him into her. It was what she wanted. As ruthless as he, she sought to drag him away from his control.

The bed was like a battlefield, full of fire and smoke and passions. The spread was soft, smooth, the air touched with spring, but it meant nothing to them. Warm flesh and sharp needs, rippling muscle and rough hands. That was their world. Her breath caught, not in fear, not in protest, but in excitement, as he pulled the robe down her body. When her arms were pinned she used her mouth as a weapon to drive him beyond reason. Her hips arched, pressing against him, tormenting, tempting, thrilling. As his hands moved over her, her strength seemed to double to race with her needs.

But here in this fuming, incendiary world there would be no winner and no loser. The fire sprinted along her skin, leaving dull, tingling aches wherever his hands or lips had touched. She wanted it, reveled in it, even while she burned for more. Not content to leave the control in his hands for long, A.J. rolled on top of him and began her own siege.

He'd never known a woman could make him shudder. He'd never known a woman could make him hurt from desire alone. She was long and limber and as ravenous as he. She was naked but not vulnerable. She was passionate but not pliant. He could see her in the moonlight, her hair pale and tumbled around her face, her skin glowing from exhilaration and needs not yet met. Her hands were soft as they raked over him, but demanding enough, bold enough, to take his breath away. The lips that followed them did nothing to soothe. She yanked his slacks down with a wild impatience that had his mind spinning and his body pounding. Then before he could react, she was sprawled across him, tasting his flesh.

It was madness. He welcomed it. It was torment. He could have begged for more. Once he'd thought he had discovered a simmering, latent passion in her, but nothing had prepared him for this. She was seduction, she was lust, she was greed. With both hands in her hair, he dragged her mouth to his so that he could taste them all.

It wasn't a dream, she thought dazedly as his mouth clung to hers and his hands again took possession. No dream had ever been so tempestuous. Reality had never been so mad. Tangled with her, he rolled her to her back. Even as she gasped for air, he plunged into her so that her body arched up, taut with the first uncontrollable climax. She reached up, too stunned to realize how badly she needed to hold on to him. Wrapped tight, their strengths fed each other as surely as their hungers did.

They lay together, weak, sated, both of them vanquished.

Gradually sanity returned. A.J. saw the moonlight again. His face was buried in her hair, but his breathing had steadied, as hers had. Her arms were still around him, her body locked tight to his. She told herself to let go, to reestablish distance, but lacked the will to obey.

It had only been passion, she reminded herself. It had only been need. Both had been satisfied. Now was the time to draw away, to move apart. But she wanted to nuzzle her cheek against his, to murmur something foolish and stay just as she was until the sun came up. With her eyes closed tight she fought the urge to soften, to give that which, once given, was lost.

No, he'd never known a woman could make him shudder. He'd never known a woman could make him weak. Yes, once he'd thought he'd discovered a simmering, latent passion in her, but he hadn't expected this. He shouldn't still feel so dazed. So involved.

He hadn't been prepared for the intensity of feeling. He hadn't planned on having the need grow and multiply even after it was satisfied. That was the reason he'd lost some part of himself to her. That was, had to be, the only reason.

But when she trembled, he drew her closer.

"Cold?"

"The air's cooled." It sounded reasonable. It sounded true. How could she explain that her body was still pumping with heat, and would be as long as he was there?

"I can shut the windows."

"No." She could hear the stream again, just smell the hyacinths. She didn't want to lose the sensations.

"Here, then." He drew away to untangle the sheets and pull them over her. It was then, in the dim light, that he noticed the pale line of smudges along her arm. Taking her elbow, he looked closer.

"Apparently I wasn't careful enough with you."

A.J. glanced down. There was regret in his voice, and a trace of a kindness she would have little defense against. If she hadn't been afraid, she would have longed to hear him speak just like that again, she would have rested her head on his shoulder. Instead, with a shrug she shifted and drew her arm away. "No permanent damage." She hoped. "I wouldn't be surprised if you found a few bruises on yourself."

He looked at her again and grinned in a way that was completely unexpected and totally charming. "It seems we both play rough."

It was too late to hold back a response to the grin. On impulse, A.J. leaned over and took a quick, none too gentle nip at his shoulder. "Complaining?"

She'd surprised him again. Maybe it was time for a few surprises in his life. And in hers. "I won't if you won't." Then, in a move too abrupt to evade, he rolled over her again, pinning her arms above her head with one hand.

"Look, Brady—"

"I like the idea of going one on one with you, A.J." He lowered his head just enough to nibble on her earlobe, until she squirmed under him.

"As long as you have the advantage." Her voice was breathy, her cheeks flushed. With his hands on her wrists he could feel the gradual acceleration of her pulse. With his body stretched full length, he could feel the dips, the curves, the fluid lines of hers. Desire began to rise again as though it had never been quenched.

"Lady, I think I might enjoy taking advantage of you on a regular basis. I know I'm going to enjoy it for the rest of the night."

She twisted one way, twisted the other, then let out a hissing breath, as he only stared down at her. Being outdone physically was nearly as bad as being outdone intellectually. "I can't stay here tonight."

"You are here," he pointed out, then took his free hand in one long stroke from her hip to her breast.

"I can't stay."

"Why?"

Because relieving pent-up passion with him and spending the night with him were two entirely different things. "Because I have to work tomorrow," she began lamely. "And—"

"I'll drop you by your apartment in the morning so you can change." The tip of her breast was already hard against his palm. He ran his thumb over it and watched passion darken her eyes.

"I have to be in the office by eight-thirty."

"We'll get up early." He lowered his head to brush kisses at either side of her mouth. "I'm not planning on getting much sleep, anyway."

Her body was a mass of nerve endings waiting to be exploited. Exploitation led to weakness, she reminded herself. And weakness to losses. "I don't spend the night with men."

"You do with this one." He brought his hand up, tracing as he went until he cupped her throat.

If she was going to lose, she'd lose with her eyes open. "Why?"

He could have given her quiet, persuasive answers. And they might have been true. Perhaps that's why he chose another way. "We haven't nearly finished with each other yet, Aurora. Not nearly."

He was right. The need was screaming through her. That she could accept. But she wouldn't accept being pressured, being cajoled or being seduced. Her terms, A.J. told herself. Then she could justify this first concession. "Let go of my hands, Brady."

Her chin was angled, her eyes direct, her voice firm. She wasn't a woman, he decided, who could be anticipated. Lifting a brow, he released her hands and waited.

With her eyes on his, she brought them to his face. Slowly her lips curved. Whether it was challenge or surrender he didn't care. "I wouldn't plan to sleep at all tonight," she warned just before she pulled his mouth to hers.

The room was still dark when A.J. roused from a light doze to draw the covers closer. There was an ache, more pleasant than annoying, in her muscles. She stretched, then shifted to glance at the luminous dial of her clock. It wasn't there. With her mind fogged with sleep, she rubbed a hand over her eyes and looked again.

Of course it wasn't there, she remembered. She wasn't there. Her clock, her apartment and her own bed were miles away. Turning again, she saw that the bed beside her was empty. Where could he have gone? she wondered as she pushed herself up. And what time was it?

She'd lost time. Hours, days, weeks, it hadn't mattered. But now she was alone, and it was time for reality again.

They'd exhausted each other, depleted each other and fed each other. She hadn't known there could be anything like the night they'd shared. Nothing real had ever been so exciting, so wild or desperate. Yet it had been very real. Her body bore the marks his hands had made while he'd been lost in passion. His taste still lingered on her tongue, his scent on her skin. It had been real, but it hadn't been reality. Reality was now, when she had to face the morning.

What she'd given, she'd given freely. She would have no regrets there. If she'd broken one of her own rules, she'd done so consciously and with deliberation. Not coolly, perhaps, but not carelessly. Neither could she be careless now. The night was over.

Because there was nothing else, A.J. picked his robe up off the floor and slipped into it. The important thing was not to be foolish, but mature. She wouldn't cuddle and cling and pretend there had been anything more between them than sex. One night of passion and mutual need.

She turned her cheek into the collar of the robe and let it linger there for a moment where his scent had permeated the cloth. Then, securing the belt, she walked out of the bedroom and down the stairs.

The living room was in shadows, but the first tongues of light filtered through the wide glass windows. David stood there, looking out, while a fire, freshly kindled, crackled beside him. A.J. felt the distance between them was like a crater, deep, wide and jagged. It took her too long to remind herself that was what she'd expected and wanted. Rather than speak, she walked the rest of the way down the stairs and waited.

"I had the place built with this window facing east so I could watch the sun rise." He lifted a cigarette and drew deep so that the tip glowed in the half-light. "No matter how many times I see it, it's different."

She wouldn't have judged him as a man drawn to sunrises. She hadn't judged him as a man who would choose a secluded house in the hills. Just how much, A.J. wondered, did she know about the man she'd spent the night with? Thrusting her hands into the pockets of the robe, her fingers brushed cardboard. A.J. curled them around the matchbook he'd stuck in there and forgotten. "I don't take much time for sunrises."

"If I happen to be right here at the right time, I usually find I can handle whatever crises the day has planned a little better."

Her fingers closed and opened, opened and closed on the matchbook. "Are you expecting any particular crisis today?"

He turned then to look at her, standing barefoot and a bit hollow eyed in his robe. It didn't dwarf her; she was only inches shorter than he. Still, somehow it made her appear more feminine, more... accessible, he decided, than anything else he remembered. It wouldn't be possible to tell her that it had just occurred to him that he was already in the middle of a crisis. Its name was Aurora J. Fields. "You know..." He tucked his hands in the back pockets of well-broken-in jeans before he took a step closer. "We didn't spend too much time talking last night."

"No." She braced herself. "It didn't seem that conversation was what either of us wanted." Nor was it conversation she'd prepared herself to deal with. "I'm going to go up and change. I do have to be in the office early."

"Aurora." He didn't reach out to stop her this time. He only had to speak. "What did you feel that first day with me in your office?"

After letting out a long breath, she faced him again. "David, I talked about that part of my life more than I cared to last night."

He knew that was true. He'd spent some time wondering why without finding any answers. She had them. If he had to probe and prod until she gave them up, he would. "You talked about it in connection with other people, other things. This happens to involve me."

"I'm going to be late for work," she murmured, and started up the landing.

"You make a habit of running away, Aurora."

"I'm not running." She whirled back, both hands clenched into fists in the pockets. "I simply don't see any reason to drag this all up again. It's personal. It's mine."

"And it touches me," he added calmly. "You walked into my bedroom last night and said you'd dreamed it. Had you?"

"I don't—" She wanted to deny it, but she had never been comfortable with direct lies. The fact that she couldn't use one had anger bubbling through. "Yes. Dreams aren't as easily controlled as conscious thought."

"Tell me what you dreamed."

She wouldn't give him all. A.J.'s nails dug into her palms. She'd be damned if she'd give him all. "I dreamed about your room. I could have described it for you before I'd ever gone in. Would you like to put me under a microscope now or later?"

"Self-pity isn't attractive." As her breath hissed out he stepped onto the landing with her. "You knew we were going to be lovers."

Her expression became cool, almost disinterested. "Yes."

"And you knew that day in your office when you were angry with me, frustrated with your mother, and our hands met, like this." He reached out, uncurled her fist and pressed their hands palm to palm.

Her back was against the wall, her hand caught in his. She was tired, spitting tired, of finding herself in corners. "What are you trying to prove, a theory for your documentary?"

What would she say if he told her he'd come to understand she showed her fangs only where she was most vulnerable? "You knew," he repeated, letting the venom spill off of him. "And it frightened you. Why was that?"

"I'd just had a strong, physical premonition that I was going to be the lover of a man I'd already decided was detestable. Is that reason enough?"

"For annoyance, even anger. Not for fear. You were afraid that night in the back of the limo, and again last night when you walked into the bedroom."

She tried to jerk her arm aside. "You're exaggerating."

"Am I?" He stepped closer and touched a hand to her cheek. "You're afraid now."

"That's not true." Deliberately she unclenched her other hand. "I'm annoyed because you're pressing me. We're adults who spent the night together. That doesn't give you the right to pry into my personal life or feelings."

No, it didn't. That was his own primary rule and he was breaking it. Somehow he'd forgotten that he had no rights, could expect none. "All right, that's true. But I saw the condition you were in yesterday afternoon after walking into that room."

"That's done," she said quickly, maybe too quickly. "There's no need to get into it again."

Though he was far from convinced, he let it ride. "And I listened to you last night. I don't want to be responsible for anything like that happening to you again."

"You're not responsible—I am." Her voice was calmer now. Emotions clouded things. She'd spent years discovering that. "You don't cause anything, I do, or if you like, circumstances do. David, I'm twenty-eight, and I've managed to survive this—something extra all my life."

"I understand that. You should understand that I'm thirty-six. I haven't been personally exposed to any of this up until a few weeks ago."

"I do understand." Her voice chilled, just a little. "And I understand the natural reaction is to be wary, curious or skeptical. The same way one looks at a side show in the circus."

"Don't put words in my mouth." His anger came as a surprise to both of them. So much of a surprise, that when he grabbed A.J. by the shoulders, she offered no protest at all. "I can't help what reaction other people have had to you. They weren't me. Damn it, I've just spent the night making love to you and I don't even know who you are. I'm afraid to touch you, thinking I might set something off. I can't keep my hands off you. I came down here this morning because if I'd lain beside you another minute I'd have taken you again while you were half-asleep."

Before she'd had a chance to weigh her own reaction, she lifted her hands up to his. "I don't know what you want."

"Neither do I." He caught himself and relaxed his grip on her. "And that's a first. Maybe I need some time to figure it out."

Time. Distance. She reminded herself that was for the best. With a nod, she dropped her hands again. "That's reasonable."

"But what isn't is that I don't want to spend that time away from you."

Chills, anxiety or excitement, rushed up her spine. "David, I—"

"I've never had a night like the one I had with you."

The weakness came quickly, to be just as quickly fought back. "You don't have to say that."

"I know I don't." With a half laugh he rubbed his hands over the shoulders he'd just clenched. "In fact, it isn't very easy to admit it. It just happens to be true, for me. Sit down a minute." He drew her down to sit on the step beside him. "I didn't have a lot of time to think last night because I was too busy being . . . stunned," he decided. She didn't relax when he put his arm around her, but she didn't draw away. "I've packed a lot of thinking into the past hour. There's more to you, A.J., than there is to a lot of other women. Even without the something extra. I think what I want is to have a chance to get to know the woman I intend to spend a lot of time making love with."

She turned to look at him. His face was close, his arm more gentle than she'd come to expect. He didn't look like a man who had any gentleness in him, only power and confidence. "You're taking a lot for granted."

"Yeah, I am."

"I don't think you should."

"Maybe not. I want you—you want me. We can start with that."

That was simpler. "No promises."

The protest sprang to his mind so quickly it stunned him. "No promises," he agreed, reminding himself that had always been rule number two.

She knew she shouldn't agree. The smart thing, the safe thing to do, was to cut things off now. One night, passion only. But she found herself relaxing against him. "Business and personal relationships completely separate."

"Absolutely."

"And when one of us becomes uncomfortable with the way things are going, we back off with no scenes or bad feelings."

"Agreed. Want it in writing?"

Her lips curved slightly as she studied him. "I should. Producers are notoriously untrustworthy."

"Agents are notoriously cynical."

"Cautious," she corrected, but lifted a hand to rub it along the stubble on his cheek. "We're paid to be the bad guys, after all. And speaking of which, we never finished discussing Clarissa."

"It isn't business hours," he reminded her, then turned her hand palm up and pressed his lips to it.

"Don't try to change the subject. We need to iron this out. Today."

"Between nine and five," he agreed.

"Fine, call my office and . . . Oh, my God."

"What?"

"My messages." Dragging both hands through her hair, she sprang up. "I never called in for my messages."

"Sounds like a national emergency," he murmured as he stood beside her.

"I was barely in the office two hours. As it was I had to reschedule appointments. Where's the phone?"

"Make it worth my while."

"David, I'm not joking."

"Neither am I." Smiling down at her, he slipped his hand into the opening of the robe and parted it. She felt her legs liquefy from the knees down.

"David." She turned her head to avoid his lips, then found herself in deeper trouble as her throat was undefended. "It'll only take me a minute."

"You're wrong." He unfastened the belt. "It's going to take longer than that."

"For all I know I might have a breakfast meeting."

"For all you know you don't have an appointment until noon." Her hands were moving down his back, under his shirt. He wondered if she was aware. "What we both know is that we should make love. Right now."

"After," she began, but sighed against his lips.

"Before."

The robe fell to the floor at her feet. Negotiations ended.

Chapter Eight

A.J. should have been satisfied. She should have been relaxed. In the ten days following her first night with David, their relationship had run smoothly. When her schedule and his allowed, they spent the evening together. There were simple evenings walking the beach, elegant evenings dining out and quiet evenings dining in. The passion that had pulled them together didn't fade. Rather, it built and intensified, driving them to quench it. He wanted her, as completely, as desperately as a man could want a woman. Of the multitude of things she was uncertain of, she could be absolutely certain of that.

She should have been relaxed. She was tied up in knots.

Each day she had to rebuild a defense that had always been like a second skin. Each night David ripped it away again. She couldn't afford to leave her emotions unprotected in what was, by her own description, a casual, physical affair. They would continue seeing each other as long as both of them enjoyed it. No promises, no commitments. When he decided to pull away, she needed to be ready.

It was, she discovered, like waiting for the other shoe to drop. He would undoubtedly break things off sooner or later. Passions that flamed too hot were bound to burn themselves out, and they had little else. He read thick, socially significant novels and informative nonfiction. A.J. leaned toward slim, gory mysteries and glitzy bestsellers. He took her to a foreign film festival full of symbolism and subtitles. She'd have chosen the Gene Kelly–Judy Garland classic on late night TV.

The more they got to know each other, the more distance A.J. saw. Passion was the magnet that drew them together, but she was very aware its power would fade. For her own survival, she intended to be prepared when it did.

On a business level she had to be just as prepared to deal with David Brady, producer. A.J. was grateful that in this particular relationship she knew every step and every angle. After listening to David's ideas for expanding Clarissa's role in the documentary, she'd agreed to the extra shoots. For a price. It hadn't been money she'd wanted to wheedle out of him, but the promise of promotion for Clarissa's next book, due out in midsummer.

It had taken two days of heated negotiations, tossing the ball back and forth, refusals, agreements and compromises. Clarissa would have her promotion directly on the program, and a review on *Book Talk*, the intellectual PBS weekly. David would have his extra studio shoots and his interview with Clarissa and Alice Van Camp. Both had walked away from the negotiating table smug that they had out done the other.

Clarissa couldn't have cared less. She was busy with her plants, her recipes and, to A.J.'s mounting dismay, her wedding plans. She took the news of the promotions A.J. had sweated for with an absent "That's nice, dear," and wondered out loud if she should bake the wedding cake herself.

"Momma, a review on *Book Talk* isn't just nice." A.J. swung into the studio parking lot frustrated from the forty-minute drive during which she and Clarissa had talked at cross purposes.

"Oh, I'm sure it's going to be lovely. The publisher said they were sending advance copies. Aurora, do you think a garden wedding would be suitable? I'm afraid my azaleas might fade.''

Brows lowered, she swung into a parking spot. "How many advance copies?''

"Oh, I'm really not sure. I probably wrote it down somewhere. And then it might rain. The weather's so unpredictable in June.''

"Make sure they send at least three. One for the— June?'' Her foot slipped off the clutch, so that the car bucked to a halt. "But that's next month.''

"Yes, and I have dozens of things to do. Just dozens.''

A.J.'s hands were very still on the wheel as she turned. "But didn't you say something about a fall wedding?''

"I suppose I did. You know my mums are at their best in October, but Alex is..." She flushed and cleared her throat. "A bit impatient. Aurora, I know I don't drive, but I think you've left your key on.''

Muttering, she pulled it out. "Momma, you're talking about marrying a man you'll have known for less than two months.''

"Do you really think time's so important?'' she asked with a sweet smile. "It's more a matter of feelings.''

"Feelings can change.'' She thought of David, of herself.

"There aren't any guarantees in life, darling.'' Clarissa reached over to cover her daughter's hand with her own. "Not even for people like you and me.''

"That's what worries me.'' She was going to talk to Alex Marshall, A.J. promised herself as she pushed her door open. Her mother was acting like a teenager going steady with the football hero. Someone had to be sensible.

"You really don't have to worry,'' Clarissa told her as she stepped onto the curb. "I know what I'm doing—really, I do. But talk to Alex by all means.''

"Momma." With a long sigh, A.J. linked arms. "I do have to worry. And mind reading's not allowed."

"I hardly have to when it's written all over your face. Is my hair all right?"

A.J. turned to kiss her cheek. "You look beautiful."

"Oh, I hope so." Clarissa gave a nervous laugh as they approached the studio doors. "I'm afraid I've become very vain lately. But Alex is such a handsome man, isn't he?"

"Yes," A.J. agreed cautiously. He was handsome, polished smooth and personable. She wouldn't be satisfied until she found the flaws.

"Clarissa." They'd hardly stepped inside, when Alex came striding down the hall. He looked like a man approaching a lost and valued treasure. "You look beautiful."

He had both of Clarissa's hands and looked to A.J. as though he would scoop her mother up and carry her off. "Mr. Marshall." She kept her voice cool and deliberately extended her own hand.

"Ms. Fields." With obvious reluctance, he released one of Clarissa hands to take A.J.'s. "I have to say you're more dedicated than my own agent. I was hoping to bring Clarissa down myself today."

"Oh, she likes to fuss," Clarissa put in, hoping to mollify them both. "And I'm afraid I'm so scatterbrained she has to remind me of all the little things about television interviews."

"Just relax," A.J. told her. "I'll go see if everything's set." Checking her watch as she went, she reached out to push open the thick studio doors, when David walked through.

"Good morning, Ms. Fields." The formal greeting was accompanied by the trail of his fingers over her wrist. "Sitting in again today?"

"Looking after my client, Brady. She's..." When she glanced casually over her shoulder, the words slipped back down her throat. There in the middle of the hallway was her mother caught up in a close and very passionate embrace. Stunned, she stared while dozens of feelings she couldn't identify ran through her.

"Your client appears to be well looked after," David murmured. When she didn't reply, he pulled her into a room off the hall. "Want to sit down?"

"No. No, I should—"

"Mind your own business."

Anger replaced shock very quickly. "She happens to be my mother."

"That's right." He walked to a coffee machine and poured two plastic cups. "Not your ward."

"I'm not going to stand by while she, while she—"

"Enjoys herself?" he suggested, and handed her the coffee.

"She isn't thinking." A.J. downed half the coffee in one swallow. "She's just riding on emotion, infatuation. And she's—"

"In love."

A.J. drank the rest of the coffee, then heaved the cup in the direction of the trash. "I hate it when you interrupt me."

"I know." And he grinned at her. "Why don't we have a quiet evening tonight, at your place? We can start making love in the living room, work our way through to the bedroom and back out again."

"David, Clarissa is my mother and I'm very concerned about her. I should—"

"Be more concerned with yourself." He had his hands on her hips. "And me." They slid firm and strong up her back. "You should be very concerned with me."

"I want you to—"

"I'm becoming an expert on what you want." His mouth brushed hers, retreated, then brushed again. "Do you know your breath starts trembling whenever I do that." His voice lowered, seductive, persuading. "Then your body begins to tremble."

Weak, weaker than she should have been, she lifted both hands to his chest. "David, we have an agreement. It's business hours."

"Sue me." He kissed her again, tempting, teasing as he slipped his hands under her jacket. "What are you wearing under here, A.J.?"

"Nothing important." She caught herself swaying forward. "David, I mean it. We agreed." His tongue traced her bottom lip. "No mixing—ah—no mixing business and...oh, damn." She forgot business and agreements and responsibilities, dragging his mouth to hers.

They filled her, those wild, wanton cravings only he could bring. They tore at her, the needs, the longings, the wishes she knew could never be met. In a moment of abandon she tossed aside what should be and groped blindly for what might be.

His mouth was as hard, as ravenous, as it had been the first time. Desire hadn't faded. His hands were as strong, as possessive and demanding as ever. Passion hadn't dimmed. It didn't matter that the room was small and smelled of old coffee and stale cigarettes. Their senses were tangled around each other. Perfume was strong and sweet; tastes were dark and exotic.

Her arms were around his neck; her fingers were raking through his hair. Her mouth was hungry and open on his.

"Oh, excuse me." Clarissa stood in the doorway, eyes lowered as she cleared her throat. It wouldn't do to look too pleased, she knew. Just as it wouldn't be wise to mention that the vibrations bouncing around in the little room might have melted lead. "I thought you'd like to know they're ready for me."

Fumbling for dignity, A.J. tugged at her jacket. "Good. I'll be right in." She waited until the door shut, then swore pungently.

"You're even," David said lightly. "You caught her—she caught you."

Her eyes, when they met his, were hot enough to sear off a layer of skin. "It's not a joke."

"Do you know one thing I've discovered about you these past few days, A.J.? You take yourself too seriously."

"Maybe I do." She scooped her purse from the sofa, then stood there nervously working the clasp. "But has it occurred to you what would have happened if a member of the crew had opened that door?"

"They'd have seen their producer kissing a very attractive woman."

"They would have seen you kissing me during a shoot. That's totally unprofessional. Before the first coffee break, everyone in the studio would be passing around the gossip."

"So?"

"So?" Exasperated, she could only stare at him. "David, that's precisely what we agreed we didn't want. We don't want your crew or our associates speculating and gossiping about our personal relationship."

Brow lifted, eyes narrowed attentively, he listened. "I don't recall discussing that in detail."

"Of course we did." She tucked her purse under her arm, then wished she still had something in her hands. "Right at the beginning."

"As I recall, the idea was to keep our personal and professional lives separate."

"That's just what I've said."

"I didn't take that to mean you wanted to keep the fact that we're lovers a secret."

"I don't want an ad in *Variety*."

He stuck his hands in his pockets. He couldn't have said why he was angry, only that he was. "You don't leave much middle ground, do you?"

She opened her mouth to spit at him, then subsided. "I guess not." On a long breath, she took a step forward. "I want to avoid the speculation, just as I want to avoid the looks of sympathy when things change."

It didn't require telepathy to understand that she'd been waiting for the change—no, he corrected, for the end—since the beginning. Knowledge brought an unexpected, and very unwelcome, twinge of pain. "I see. All right, then, we'll try it your way." He walked to the door and held it open. "Let's go punch in."

No, he couldn't have said why he was angry. In fact, he knew he shouldn't have been. A.J.'s ground rules were logical, and if anything, they made things easier for him. Or should have made things easier for him. She made absolutely no demands and accepted none. In other relationships he'd insisted on the same thing. She refused to allow emotions to interfere with her business or his. In the past he'd felt precisely the same way.

The problem was, he didn't feel that way now.

As the shoot ground to a halt because of two defective bulbs David reminded himself it was his problem. Once he accepted that, he could work on the solution. One was to go along with the terms. The other was to change them.

David watched A.J. cross the room toward Alex. Her stride was brisk, her eyes cool. In the conservative suit she looked like precisely what she was—a successful business-woman who knew where she was going and how to get there. He remembered the way she looked when they made love—slim, glowing and as dangerous as a neutron bomb.

David took out a cigarette then struck a match with a kind of restrained violence. He was going to have to plan out solution number two.

"Mr. Marshall." A.J. had her speech prepared and her determination at its peak. With a friendly enough smile, she interrupted Alex's conversation with one of the grips. "Could I speak with you for a minute?"

"Of course." Because he'd been expecting it, Alex took her arm in his innate old-style manner. "Looks like we'll have time for a cup of coffee."

Together they walked back to the room where A.J. had stood with David a few hours before. This time she poured the coffee and offered the cup. But before she could start the prologue for the speech she'd been rehearsing, Alex began.

"You want to talk about Clarissa." He pulled out one of his cigars, then held it out. "Do you mind?"

"No, go ahead. Actually, Mr. Marshall, I would very much like to talk to you about Clarissa."

"She told me you were uneasy about our marriage plans." He puffed comfortably on his cigar until he was satisfied it was well started. "I admit that puzzled me a bit, until she explained that besides being her agent, you happen to be her daughter. Shall we sit down?"

A.J. frowned at the sofa, then at him. It wasn't going at all according to plan. She took her place on one end, while he settled himself on the other. "I'm glad that Clarissa explained things to you. It simplifies things. You'll understand now why I'm concerned. My mother is very important to me."

"And to me." As he leaned back, A.J. studied his profile. It wasn't difficult to see why her mother was infatuated. "You of all people can understand just how easy Clarissa is to love."

"Yes." A.J. sipped at her coffee. What was it she'd planned to say? Taking a deep breath, she moved back on track. "Clarissa is a wonderfully warm and very special person. The thing is, you've known each other for such a short time."

"It only took five minutes." He said it so simply, A.J. was left fumbling for words. "Ms. Fields," he continued, then smiled at her. "A.J.," he corrected. "It doesn't seem right for me to call you 'Ms. Fields.' After all, I'm going to be your stepfather."

Stepfather? Somehow that angle had bypassed her. She sat, coffee cup halfway to her lips, and stared at him.

"I have a son your age," he began again. "And a daughter not far behind. I think I understand some of what you're feeling."

"It's, ah, it's not a matter of my feelings."

"Of course it is. You're as precious to Clarissa as my children are to me. Clarissa and I will be married, but she'd be happier if you were pleased about it."

A.J. frowned at her coffee, then set it down. "I don't know what to say. I thought I did. Mr. Marshall, Alex, you've been a journalist for over a quarter of a century. You've traveled all over the world, seen incredible things. Clarissa, for all her abilities, all her insights, is a very simple woman."

"An amazingly comfortable woman, especially for a man who's lived on the edge, perhaps too long. I had thought of retiring." He laughed then, but comfortably, as he remembered his own shock when Clarissa had held his hand and commented on it. "That wasn't something I'd discussed with anyone, not even my own children. I'd been looking for something more, something other than deadlines and breaking stories. In a matter of hours after being with Clarissa, I knew she was what I'd been looking for. I want to spend the rest of my life with her."

A.J. sat in silence, looking down at her hands. What more could a woman ask for, she wondered, than for a man to love her with such straightforward devotion? Couldn't a woman consider herself fortunate to have a man who accepted who she was, what she was, and loved her because of it, not in spite of?

Some of the tension dissolved and as she looked up at him she was able to smile. "Alex, has my mother fixed you dinner?"

"Why, yes." Though his tone was very sober, she caught, and appreciated, the gleam in his eyes. "Several times. In fact, she told me she's left a pot of spaghetti sauce simmering for tonight. I find Clarissa's cooking as—unique as she is."

With a laugh, A.J. held out her hand again. "I think Momma hit the jackpot." He took her hand, then surprised her by leaning over to kiss her cheek.

"Thank you."

"Don't hurt her," A.J. whispered. She clung to his hand a moment, then composing herself rose. "We'd better get back. She'll wonder where we are."

"Being Clarissa I'm sure she has a pretty good idea."

"That doesn't bother you?" She stopped by the door to look up at him again. "The fact that she's a sensitive?"

"Why should it? That's part of what makes Clarissa who she is."

"Yes." She tried not to think of herself, but didn't bite back the sigh in time. "Yes, it is."

When they walked back into the studio Clarissa looked over immediately. It only took a moment before she smiled. In an old habit, A.J. kissed both her cheeks. "There is one thing I have to insist on," she began without preamble.

"What is it?"

"That I give you the wedding."

Pleasure bloomed on Clarissa's cheeks even as she protested. "Oh, darling, how sweet, but it's too much trouble."

"It certainly is for a bride. You pick out your wedding dress and your trousseau and worry about looking terrific. I'll handle the rest." She kissed her again. "Please."

"If you really want to."

"I really want to. Give me a guest list and I'll handle the details. That's what I'm best at. I think they want you." She gave Clarissa a last quick squeeze before urging her back on set. A.J. took her place in the background.

"Feeling better?" David murmured as he came up beside her.

"Some." She couldn't admit to him that she felt weepy and displaced. "As soon as the shoot's finished, I start making wedding plans."

"Tomorrow's soon enough." When she sent him a puzzled look, he only smiled. "I intend to keep you busy this evening."

He was a man of his word. A.J. had barely arrived home, shed her jacket and opened the phone book to *Caterers*, when the bell rang. Taking the book with her, she went to answer. "David." She hooked her finger in the page so as not to lose her place. "You told me you had some things to do."

"I did them. What time is it?"

"It's quarter to seven. I didn't think you'd be by until around eight."

"Well after business hours then." He toyed with, then loosened the top button of her blouse.

She had to smile. "Well after."

"And if you don't answer your phone, your service will pick it up after four rings?"

"Six. But I'm not expecting any calls." She stepped closer to slide her arms up his chest. "Hungry?"

"Yeah." He tested himself, seeing how long he could hold her at arm's length. It appeared to be just over thirty seconds.

"There's nothing in the kitchen except a frozen fish dinner." She closed her eyes as his lips skimmed over her jaw.

"Then we'll have to find another way to satisfy the appetite." He unhooked her skirt and, as it fell to the floor, drew his hands down her hips.

She yanked his sweater over his head and tossed it aside. "I'm sure we'll manage."

His muscles were tight as she ran her hands over his. Taut, tense all the way from his neck to his waist. With her blouse half-open, her legs clad in sheer stockings that stopped just at her thighs, A.J. pressed against him. She wanted to make him burn with just the thought of loving her. Then she was gasping for air, her fingers digging into his back as his hands took quick and complete possession.

When her legs buckled and she went limp against him he didn't relent. For hours and hours he'd held back, watching her sit primly in the back of the studio, looking at her make her precise notes in her book. Now he had her, alone, hot, moist and, for the first time in their lovemaking, weak.

Holding her close, he slid with her to the floor.

Unprepared, she was helpless against a riot of sensation. He took her on a desperate ride, driving her up where the air was thin, plunging her down where it was heavy and dark. She tried to cling to him but lacked the strength.

She trembled for him. That alone was enough to drive him mad. His name came helplessly through her lips. He wanted to hear it, again and again, over and over. He wanted to know she thought of nothing else. And when he pulled the remaining clothes from both of them, when he entered her with a violence neither of them could fight, he knew he thought of nothing but her.

She shuddered again and again, but he held himself back from ultimate release. Even as he drove her, his hands continued to roam, bringing unspeakable pleasures to every inch of her body. The carpet was soft at her back, but even when her fingers curled into it she could only feel the hard thrust of her lover. She heard him say her name, once, then twice, until her eyes fluttered open. His body rose above hers, taut with muscle, gleaming from passion. His breath was heaving even as hers was. She heard it, then tasted it when his mouth crushed down to devour. Then she heard nothing but her own sobbing moan as they emptied themselves.

"I like you naked." When he'd recovered enough, David propped himself on his elbow and took a long, long look. "But I have to admit, I'm fascinated by those little stockings you wear that stop right about here." To demonstrate, he ran his fingertip along her upper thigh.

Still dazed, A.J. merely moved against his touch. "They're very practical."

With a muffled laugh, he nuzzled the side of her neck. "Yes, that's what fascinates me. Your practicality."

She opened her eyes but kept them narrowed. "That's not what I meant." Because she felt too good to make an issue of it, she curled into him.

It was one of the things that charmed him most. David wondered if he told her how soft, how warm and open to affection she was after loving, if she would pull back. Instead he held her close, stroking and pleasing them both. When he caught himself half dozing, he pulled her up.

"Come on, let's have a shower before dinner."

"A shower?" She let her head rest on his shoulder. "Why don't we just go to bed."

"Insatiable," he decided, and scooped her up.

"David, you can't carry me."

"Why not?"

"Because." She groped. "Because it's silly."

"I always feel silly carrying naked women." In the bathroom, he stood her on her feet.

"I suppose you make a habit of it," she commented dryly, and turned on the taps with a hard twist.

"I have been trying to cut down." Smiling, he pulled her into the shower with him so that the water rained over her face.

"My hair!" She reached up once, ineffectually to block the flow, then stopped to glare at him.

"What about it?"

"Never mind." Resigned, she picked up the soap and began to rub it lazily over her body as she watched him. "You seem very cheerful tonight. I thought you were annoyed with me this morning."

"Did you?" He'd given some thoughts to strangling her. "Why would I be?" He took the soap from her and began to do the job himself.

"When we were talking…" The soap was warm and slick, his touch very thorough. "It doesn't matter. I'm glad you came by."

That was more than he'd come to expect from her. "Really?"

She smiled, then wrapped her arms around him and kissed him under the hot, steamy spray. "Yes, really. I like you, David. When you're not being a producer."

That, too, was more than he'd come to expect from her. And less than he was beginning to need. "I like you, Aurora. When you're not being an agent."

When she stepped out of the shower and reached for towels, she heard the bell ring again. "Damn." She gripped a towel at her breasts.

"I'll get it." David hooked a towel at his hips and strode out before A.J. could protest. She let out a huff of breath and snatched the robe from its hook on the door. If it was someone from the office, she'd have a lovely time explaining why David Brady, producer, was answering her door in a towel. She decided discretion was the better part of valor and stayed where she was.

Then she remembered the clothes. She closed her eyes on a moan as she imagined the carelessly strewn articles on her living room floor. Bracing herself, she walked down the hall back into the living room.

There was candlelight. On the ebony table she kept by the window, candles were already burning in silver holders on a white cloth. She saw the gleam of china, the sparkle of crystal, and stood where she was as David signed a paper handed to him by a man in a black suit.

"I hope everything is satisfactory, Mr. Brady."

"I'm sure it will be."

"We will, of course, be back for pickup at your convenience." With a bow to David, then another to A.J., he let himself out the door.

"David…" A.J. walked forward as if she weren't sure of her steps. "What is this?"

He lifted a silver cover from a plate. "It's coq au vin."

"But how did you—"

"I ordered it for eight o'clock." He checked his watch before he walked over to retrieve his pants. "They're very prompt. With the ease of a totally unself-conscious man, he dropped the towel and drew on his slacks.

She took another few steps toward the table. "It's lovely. Really lovely." There was a single rose in a vase. Moved, she reached out to touch it, then immediately brought her hand back to link it with her other. "I never expected anything like this."

He drew his sweater back over his head. "You said once you enjoyed being pampered." She looked stunned, he realized. Had he been so unromantic? A little uncertain, he walked to her. "Maybe I enjoy doing the pampering now and then."

She looked over, but her throat was closed and her eyes were filling. "I'll get dressed."

"No." Her back was to him now, but he took her by the shoulders. "No, you look fine."

She struggled with herself, pressing her lips together until she thought she could speak. "I'll just be a minute." But he was turning her around. His brows were already knit together before he saw her face.

"What's this?" He lifted a fingertip and touched a tear that clung to her lashes.

"It's nothing. I—I feel foolish. Just give me a minute."

He brushed another tear away with his thumb. "No, I don't think I should." He'd seen her weep before, but that had been a torrent. There was something soft in these tears, something incredibly sweet that drew him. "Do you always cry when a man offers you a quiet dinner?"

"No, of course not. It's just—I never expected you to do anything like this."

He brought her hand to his lips and smiled as he kissed her fingers. "Just because I'm a producer doesn't mean I can't have some class."

"That's not what I meant." She looked up at him, smiling down at her, her hands still close to his lips. She was losing. A.J. felt her heart weaken, her will weaken and her wishes grow. "That's not what I meant," she said again in a whisper, and tightened her fingers on his. "David, don't make me want too much."

It was what he thought he understood. If you wanted too much, you fell too hard. He'd avoided the same thing, maybe for the same reasons, until one late afternoon on a beach. "Do you really think either of us can stop now?"

She thought of how many times she'd been rejected, easily, coolly, nervously. Friendship, affection, love could be turned off by some as quickly as a faucet. He wanted her now, A.J. reminded herself. He cared now. It had to be enough. She touched a hand to his cheek.

"Maybe tonight we won't think at all."

Chapter Nine

"Item fifteen, clause B. I find the wording here too vague. As we discussed, my client feels very strongly about her rights and responsibilities as a new mother. The nanny will accompany the child to the set, at my client's expense. However, she will require regular breaks in order to feed the infant. The trailer provided by you must be equipped with a portable crib and...'" For the third time during her dictation, A.J. lost her train of thought.

"Diapers?" Diane suggested.

"What?" A.J. turned from the window to look at her secretary.

"Just trying to help. Want me to read it back to you?"

"Yes, please."

While Diane read the words back, A.J. frowned down at the contract in her hand. "'And a playpen,'" A.J. finished, and managed to smile at her secretary. "I've never seen anyone so wrapped up in motherhood."

"Doesn't fit her image, does it? She always plays the heartless sex bomb."

"This little movie of the week should change that. Okay, finish it up with 'Once the above changes are made, the contract will be passed along to my client for signing.'"

"Do you want this out today?"

"Hmm?"

"Today, A.J.?" With a puzzled smile, Diane studied her employer. "You want the letter to go right out?"

"Oh. Yes, yes, it'd better go out." She checked her watch. "I'm sorry, Diane, it's nearly five. I hadn't realized."

"No problem." Closing her notebook, Diane rose. "You seem a little distracted today. Big plans for the holiday weekend?"

"Holiday?"

"Memorial Day weekend, A.J." With a shake of her head, Diane tucked her pencil behind her ear. "You know, three days off, the first weekend of summer. Sand, surf, sun."

"No." She began rearranging the papers on her desk. "I don't have any plans." Shaking off the mood, she looked up again. Distracted? What she was was a mess. She was bogged down in work she couldn't concentrate on, tied up in knots she couldn't loosen. With a shake of her head, she glanced at Diane again and remembered there were other people in the world beside herself. "I'm sure you do. Let the letter wait. There's no mail delivery Monday, anyway. We'll send it over by messenger Tuesday."

"As a matter of fact, I do have an interesting three days planned." Diane gave her own watch a check. "And he's picking me up in an hour."

"Go home." A.J. waved her off as she shuffled through papers. "Don't get sunburned."

"A.J.—" Diane paused at the door and grinned "—I don't plan to see the sun for three full days."

When the door shut, A.J. slipped off her glasses and rubbed at the bridge of her nose. What was wrong with her? She couldn't seem to concentrate for more than five minutes at a stretch before her attention started wandering.

Overwork? she wondered as she looked down at the papers in her hand. That was an evasion; she thrived on overwork. She wasn't sleeping well. She was sleeping alone. One had virtually nothing to do with the other, A.J. assured herself as she unstacked and restacked papers. She was too much her own person to moon around because David Brady had been out of town for a few days.

But she did miss him. She picked up a pencil to work, then ended up merely running it through her fingers. There wasn't any crime in missing him, was there? It wasn't as though she were dependent on him. She'd just gotten used to his company. Wouldn't he be smug and self-satisfied to know that she'd spent half her waking hours thinking about him? Disgusted with herself, A.J. began to work in earnest. For two minutes.

It was his fault, she thought as she tossed the pencil down again. That extravagantly romantic dinner for two, then that silly little bouquet of daisies he'd sent the day he'd left for Chicago. Though she tried not to, she reached out and stroked the petals that sat cheerful and out of place on her desk. He was trying to make a giddy, romantic fool out of her—and he was succeeding.

It just had to stop. A.J. adjusted her glasses, picked up her pencil and began to work again. She wasn't going to give David Brady another thought. When the knock sounded at her door a few moments later, she was staring into space. She blinked herself out of the daydream, swore, then called out. "Come in."

"Don't you ever quit?" Abe asked her when he stuck his head in the door.

Quit? She'd barely made a dent. "I've got a couple of loose ends. Abe, the Forrester contract comes up for renewal the first of July. I think we should start prodding. His fan mail was two to one last season, so—"

"First thing Tuesday morning I'll put the squeeze on. Right now I have to go marinate."

"I beg your pardon?"

"Big barbecue this weekend," Abe told her with a wink. "It's the only time my wife lets me cook. Want me to put a steak on for you?"

She smiled, grateful that he'd brought simpler things to her mind. Hickory smoke, freshly cut grass, burned meat. "No, thanks. The memory of the last one's a little close."

"The butcher gave me bad quality meat." He hitched up his belt and thought about spending the whole weekend in bathing trunks.

"That's what they all say. Have a good holiday, Abe. Just be prepared to squeeze hard on Tuesday."

"No problem. Want me to lock up?"

"No, I'll just be a few more minutes."

"If you change your mind about that steak, just come by."

"Thanks." Alone again, A.J. turned her concentration back to her work. She heard the sounds of her staff leaving for the day. Doors closing, scattered laughter.

David stood in the doorway and watched her. The rest of her staff was pouring out of the door as fast as they could, but she sat, calm and efficient, behind her desk. The fatigue that had had him half dozing on the plane washed away. Her hair was tidy, her suit jacket trim and smooth over her shoulders. She held the pencil in long, ringless fingers and wrote in quick, static bursts. The daisies he'd sent her days before sat in a squat vase on her desk. It was the first, the only unbusinesslike accent he'd ever seen in her office. Seeing them made him smile. Seeing her made him want.

He could see himself taking her there in her prim organized office. He could peel that tailored, successful suit from her and find something soft and lacy beneath. With the door locked and traffic rushing by far below, he could make love with her until all the needs, all the fantasies that had built in the days he'd been away were satisfied.

A.J. continued to write, forcing her concentration back each time it threatened to ebb. It wasn't right, she told herself, that her system would start to churn this way for no reason. The dry facts and figures she was reading shouldn't leave room for hot imagination. She rubbed the back of her neck, annoyed that tension was building there out of nothing. She would have sworn she could feel passion in the air. But that was ridiculous.

Then she knew. As surely as if he'd spoken, as surely as if he'd already touched her. Slowly, her hand damp on the pencil, she looked up.

There was no surprise in her eyes. It should have made him uneasy that she'd sensed him there when he'd made no sound, no movement. The fact that it didn't was something he would think of later. Now he could only think of how cool and proper she looked behind the desk. Of how wild and wanton she was in his arms.

She wanted to laugh, to spring up from the desk and rush across the room. She wanted to be held close and swung in dizzying circles while the pleasure of just seeing him again soared through her. Of course she couldn't. That would be foolish. Instead she lifted a brow and set her pencil on her blotter. "So you're back."

"Yeah. I had a feeling I'd find you here." He wanted to drag her up from her chair and hold her. Just hold her. He dipped his hands into his pockets and leaned against the jamb.

"A feeling?" This time she smiled. "Precognition or telepathy?"

"Logic." He smiled, too, then walked toward the desk. "You look good, Fields. Real good."

Leaning back in her chair, she gave herself the pleasure of a thorough study. "You look a little tired. Rough trip?"

"Long." He plucked a daisy from the vase and spun it by the stem. "But it should be the last one before we wrap." Watching her, he came around the desk, then, resting a hip on it, leaned over and tucked the daisy behind her ear. "Got any plans for tonight?"

If she'd had any, she would have tossed them out the window and forgotten them. With her tongue caught in her teeth, A.J. made a business out of checking her desk calender. "No."

"Tomorrow?"

She flipped the page over. "Doesn't look like it."

"Sunday?"

"Even agents need a day of rest."

"Monday?"

She flipped the next page and shrugged. "Offices are closed. I thought I'd spend the day reading over some scripts and doing my nails."

"Um-hmm. In case you hadn't noticed, office hours are over."

Her heart was drumming. Already. Her blood was warming. So soon. "I'd noticed."

In silence he held out his hand. After only a slight hesitation, A.J. put hers into it and let him draw her up. "Come home with me."

He'd asked her before, and she'd refused. Looking at him now, she knew the days of refusal were long past. Reaching down, she gathered her purse and her briefcase.

"Not tonight," David told her, and took the briefcase to set it back down.

"I want to—"

"Not tonight, Aurora." Taking her hand again, he brought it to his lips. "Please."

With a nod, she left the briefcase and the office behind.

They kept their hands linked as they walked down the hall. They kept them linked still as they rode down in the elevator. It didn't seem foolish, A.J. realized, but sweet. He hadn't kissed her, hadn't held her, and yet the tension that had built so quickly was gone again, just through a touch.

She was content to leave her car in the lot, thinking that sometime the next day, they'd drive back into town and ar-range things. Pleased just to be with him again, she stopped at his car while he unlocked the doors.

"Haven't you been home yet?" she asked, noticing a suitcase in the back seat.

"No."

She started to smile, delighted that he'd wanted to see her first, but she glanced over her shoulder again as she stepped into the car. "I have a case just like that."

David settled in the seat, then turned on the ignition. "That is your case."

"Mine?" Baffled, she turned around and looked closer. "But—I don't remember you borrowing one of my suitcases."

"I didn't. Mine are in the trunk." He eased out of the lot and merged with clogged L.A. weekend traffic.

"Well, if you didn't borrow it, what's it doing in your car?"

"I stopped by your place on the way. Your housekeeper packed for you."

"Packed . . ." She stared at the case. When she turned to him, her eyes were narrowed. "You've got a lot of nerve, Brady. Just where do you come off packing my clothes and assuming—"

"The housekeeper packed them. Nice lady. I thought you'd be more comfortable over the weekend with some of your own things. I had thought about keeping you naked, but that's a little tricky when you take walks in the woods."

Because her jaw was beginning to ache, she relaxed it. "You thought? *You* didn't think at all. You drop by the office and calmly assume that I'll drop everything and run off with you. What if I'd had plans?"

"Then that would've been too bad." He swung easily off the ramp toward the hills.

"Too bad for whom?"

"For the plans." He punched in the car lighter and sent her a mild smile. "I have no intention of letting you out of my sight for the next three days."

"You have no intention?" The fire was rising as she shifted in her seat toward him. "What about my intention? Maybe you think it's very male and macho to just—just bundle a woman off for a weekend without asking, without any discussion, but I happen to prefer being consulted. Stop the car."

"Not a chance." David had expected this reaction. Even looked forward to it. He touched the lighter to the tip of his cigarette. He hadn't enjoyed himself this much for days. Since the last time he'd been with her.

Her breath came out in a long, slow hiss. "I don't find abductions appealing."

"Didn't think I did, either." He blew out a lazy stream of smoke. "Guess I was wrong."

She flopped back against her seat, arms folded. "You're going to be sorry."

"I'm only sorry I didn't think of it before." With his elbow resting lightly on the open window, he drove higher into the hills, with A.J. fuming beside him. The minute he stopped the car in his drive, A.J. pushed open her door, snatched her purse up and began to walk. When he grabbed her arm, she spun around, holding the pastel-dyed leather like a weapon.

"Want to fight?"

"I wouldn't give you the satisfaction." She yanked her arm out of his hold. "I'm walking back."

"Oh?" He look a quick look at the slim skirt, thin hose and fragile heels. "You wouldn't make it the first mile in those shoes."

"That's my problem."

He considered a minute, then sighed. "I guess we'll just carry through with the same theme." Before she realized his intention, he wrapped an arm around her waist and hauled her over his shoulder.

Too stunned to struggle, she blew hair out of her eyes. "Put me down."

"In a few minutes," he promised as he walked toward the house.

"Now." She whacked him smartly on the back with her purse. "This isn't funny."

"Are you kidding?" When he stuck his key in the lock, she began to struggle. "Easy, A.J., you'll end up dropping on your head."

"I'm not going to tolerate this." She tried to kick out and found her legs pinned behind the knee. "David, this is degrading. I don't know what's gotten into you, but if you get a hold of yourself now, I'll forget the whole thing."

"No deal." He started up the steps.

"I'll give you a deal," she said between her teeth as she made a futile grab for the railing. "If you put me down now, I won't kill you."

"Now?"

"Right now."

"Okay." With a quick twist of his body, he had her falling backward. Even as her eyes widened in shock, he was tumbling with her onto the bed.

"What the hell's gotten into you?" she demanded as she struggled to sit up.

"You," he said so simply she stopped in the act of shoving him away. "You," he repeated, cupping the back of her neck. "I thought about you the whole time I was gone. I wanted you in Chicago. I wanted you in the airport, and thirty thousand feet up I still wanted you."

"You're—this is crazy."

"Maybe. Maybe it is. But when I was on that plane flying back to L.A. I realized that I wanted you here, right here, alone with me for days."

His fingers were stroking up and down her neck, soothing. Her nerves were stretching tighter and tighter. "If you'd asked," she began.

"You'd have had an excuse. You might have spent the night." His fingers inched up into her hair. "But you'd have found a reason you couldn't stay longer."

"That's not true."

"Isn't it? Why haven't you spent a weekend with me before?"

Her fingers linked and twisted. "There've been reasons."

"Yeah." He put his hand over hers. "And the main one is you're afraid to spend more than a few hours at a time with me." When she opened her mouth, he shook his head to cut her off. "Afraid if you do, I might just get too close."

"I'm not afraid of you. That's ridiculous."

"No, I don't think you are. I think you're afraid of us." He drew her closer. "So am I."

"David." The word was shaky. The world was suddenly shaky. Just passion, she reminded herself again. That's what made her head swim, her heart pound. Desire. Her arms slid up his back. It was only desire. "Let's not think at all for a while." She touched her lips to his and felt resistance as well as need.

"Sooner or later we're going to have to."

"No." She kissed him again, let her tongue trace lightly over his lips. "There's no sooner, no later." Her breath was warm, tempting, as it fluttered over him. "There's only now. Make love with me now, in the light." Her hands slipped under his shirt to tease and invite.

Her eyes were open and on his, her lips working slowly, steadily to drive him to the edge. He swore, then pulled her to him and let the madness come.

* * *

"It's good for you."

"So's calves' liver," A.J. said breathlessly, and paused to lean against a tree. "I avoid that, too."

They'd taken the path behind his house, crossed the stream and continued up. By David's calculations they'd gone about three-quarters of a mile. He walked back to stand beside her. "Look." He spread his arm wide. "It's terrific, isn't it?"

The trees were thick and green. Birds rustled the leaves and sang for the simple pleasure of sound. Wildflowers she'd never seen before and couldn't name pushed their way through the underbrush and battled for the patches of sunlight. It was, even to a passionately avowed city girl, a lovely sight.

"Yes, it's terrific. You tend to forget there's anything like this when you're down in L.A."

"That's why I moved up here." He put an arm around her shoulder and absently rubbed his hand up and down. "I was beginning to forget there was any place other than the fast lane."

"Work, parties, meetings, parties, brunch, lunch and cocktails."

"Yeah, something like that. Anyway, coming up here after a day in the factory keeps things in perspective. If a project bombs in the ratings, the sun's still going to set."

She thought about it, leaning into him a bit as he stroked her arm. "If I blow a deal, I go home, lock the doors, put on my headset and drown my brain in Rachmaninoff."

"Same thing."

"But usually I kick something first."

He laughed and kissed the top of her head. "Whatever works. Wait till you see the view from the top."

A.J. leaned down to massage her calf. "I'll meet you back at the house. You can draw me a picture."

"You need the air. Do you realize we've barely been out of bed for thirty-six hours."

"And we've probably logged about ten hours' sleep." Straightening a bit, she stretched protesting muscles. "I think I've had enough health and nature for the day."

He looked down at her. She wasn't A. J. Fields now, in T-shirt and jeans and scuffed boots. But he still knew how to play her. "I guess I'm in better shape than you are."

"Like hell." She pushed away from the tree.

Determined to keep up, she strode along beside him, up the winding dirt path, until sweat trickled down her back. Her leg muscles whimpered, reminding her she'd neglected her weekly tennis games for over a month. At last, aching and exhausted, she dropped down on a rock.

"That's it. I give up."

"Another hundred yards and we start circling back."

"Nope."

"A.J., it's shorter to go around this way than to turn around."

Shorter? She shut her eyes and asked herself what had possessed her to let him drag her through the woods. "I'll just stay here tonight. You can bring me back a pillow and a sandwich."

"I could always carry you."

She folded her arms. "No."

"How about a bribe?"

Her bottom lip poked out as she considered. "I'm always open to negotiations."

"I've got a bottle of Cabernet-Sauvignon I've been saving for the right moment."

She rubbed at a streak of dirt on her knee. "What year?"

"Seventy-nine."

"A good start. That might get me the next hundred yards or so."

"Then there's that steak I took out of the freezer this morning, the one I'm going to grill over mesquite."

"I'd forgotten about that." She brought her tongue over her top lip and thought she could almost taste it. "That should get me halfway back down."

"You drive a hard bargain."

"Thank you."

"Flowers. Dozens of them."

She lifted a brow. "By the time we get back, the florist'll be closed."

"City oriented," he said with a sigh. "Look around you."

"You're going to pick me flowers?" Surprised, and foolishly pleased, she lifted her arms to twine them around his neck. "That should definitely get me through the front door."

Smiling, she leaned back as he stepped off the path to gather blossoms. "I like the blue ones," she called out, and laughed as he muttered at her.

She hadn't expected the weekend to be so relaxed, so easy. She hadn't known she could enjoy being with one person for so long. There were no schedules, no appointments, no pressing deals. There were simply mornings and afternoons and evenings.

It seemed absurd that something as mundane as fixing breakfast could be fun. She'd discovered that spending the time to eat it instead of rushing into the morning had a certain appeal. When you weren't alone. She didn't have a script or a business letter to deal with. And she had to admit, she hadn't missed them. She'd done nothing more mind teasing in two days than a crossword puzzle. And even that, she remembered happily, had been interrupted.

Now he was picking her flowers. Small, colorful wildflowers. She'd put them in a vase by the window where they'd be cozy and bright. And deadly.

For an instant, her heart stopped. The birds were silent and the air was still as glass. She saw David as though she were looking through a long lens. As she watched, the light went gray. There was pain, sharp and sudden, as her knuckles scraped over the rock.

"No!" She thought she shouted, but the word came out in a whisper. She nearly slipped off the rock before she caught herself and stumbled toward him. She gasped for his name twice before it finally ripped out of her. "David! No, stop."

He straightened, but only had time to take a step toward her before she threw herself into his arms. He'd seen that blank terror in her eyes before, once before, when she'd stood in an old empty room watching something no one else could see.

"Aurora, what is it?" He held her close while she shuddered, though he had no idea how to soothe. "What's wrong?"

"Don't pick any more. David, don't." Her fingers dug hard into his back.

"All right, I won't." Hands firm, he drew her away to study her face. "Why?"

"Something's wrong with them." The fear hadn't passed. She pressed the heel of her hand against her chest as if to push it out. "Something's wrong with them," she repeated.

"They're just flowers." He showed her what he held in his hands.

"Not them. Over there. You were going to pick those over there."

He followed the direction of her gaze to a large sunny rock with flowers around the perimeter. He remembered he'd just been turning in their direction when her shouts had stopped him. "Yes, I was. Let's have a look."

"No." She grabbed him again. "Don't touch them."

"Calm down," he said quietly enough, though his own nerves were starting to jangle. Bending, he picked up a stick. Letting the flowers he'd already picked fall, he took A.J.'s hand in his and dragged the end of the stick along the edge of the rock through a thick clump of bluebells. He heard the hissing rattle, felt the jolt of the stick he held as the snake reared up and struck. A.J.'s hand went limp in his. David held on to the stick as he pulled her back to the path. He wore boots, thick and sturdy enough to protect against the snakes scattered through the hills. But he'd been picking flowers, and there had been nothing to protect the vulnerable flesh of his hands and wrists.

"I want to go back," she said flatly.

She was grateful he didn't question, didn't probe or even try to soothe. If he had, she wasn't sure what idiotic answers she'd have given him. A.J. had discovered more in that one timeless moment than David's immediate danger. She'd discovered she was in love with him. All her rules, her warnings, her precautions hadn't mattered. He could hurt her now, and she might never recover.

So she didn't speak. Because he was silent, as well, she felt the first pang of rejection. They entered through the kitchen door. David took a bottle of brandy and two water glasses out of a cupboard. He poured, handed one to A.J., then emptied half the contents of his own glass in one swallow.

She sipped, then sipped again, and felt a little steadier. "Would you like to take me home now?"

He picked up the bottle and added a dollop to his glass. "What are you talking about?"

A.J. wrapped both hands around her glass and made herself speak calmly. "Most people are uncomfortable after—after an episode. They either want to distance themselves from the source or dissect it." When he said nothing, only stared at her, she set her glass down. "It won't take me long to pack."

"You take another step," he said in a voice that was deadly calm, "and I don't know what the hell I'll do. Sit down, Aurora."

"David, I don't want an interrogation."

He hurled his glass into the sink, making her jolt at the sudden violence. "Don't we know each other any better than that by now?" He was shouting. She couldn't know it wasn't at her, but himself. "Can't we have any sort of discussion, any sort of contact, that isn't sex or negotiations?"

"We agreed—"

He said something so uncharacteristically vulgar about agreements that she stopped dead. "You very possibly saved my life." He stared down at his hand, well able to imagine what might have happened. "What am I supposed to say to you? Thanks?"

When she found herself stuttering, A.J. swallowed and pulled herself back. "I'd really rather you didn't say anything."

He walked to her but didn't touch. "I can't. Look, I'm a little shaky about this myself. That doesn't mean I've suddenly decided you're a freak." He saw the emotion come and go in her eyes before he reached out to touch her face. "I'm grateful. I just don't quite know how to handle it."

"It's all right." She was losing ground. She could feel it. "I don't expect—"

"Do." He brought his other hand to her face. "Do expect. Tell me what you want. Tell me what you need right now."

She tried not to. She'd lose one more foothold if she did. But his hands were gentle when they never were, and his eyes offered. "Hold me." She closed her eyes as she said it. "Just hold me a minute."

He put his arms around her, drew her against him. There was no passion, no fire, just comfort. He felt her hands knead at his back until both of them relaxed. "Do you want to talk about it?"

"It was just a flash. I was sitting there, thinking about how nice it had been to do nothing. I was thinking about the flowers. I had a picture of them in the window. All at once they were black and ugly and the petals were like razors. I saw you bending over that clump of bluebells, and it all went gray."

"I hadn't bent over them yet."

"You would have."

"Yeah." He held her closer a moment. "I would have. Looks like I reneged on the last part of the deal. I don't have any flowers for you."

"It doesn't matter." She pressed her lips against his neck.

"I'll have to make it up to you." Drawing back, he took both of her hands. "Aurora..." He started to lift one, then saw the caked blood on her knuckles. "What the hell have you done to yourself?"

Blankly she looked down. "I don't know. It hurts," she said as she flexed her hand.

"Come on." He led her to the sink and began to clean off dried blood with cool water.

"Ow!" She would have jerked her hand away if he hadn't held it still.

"I've never had a very gentle touch," he muttered.

She leaned a hip against the sink. "So I've noticed."

Annoyed at seeing the rough wound on her hand, he began to dab it with a towel. "Let's go upstairs. I've got some Merthiolate."

"That stings."

"Don't be a baby."

"I'm not." But he had to tug her along. "It's only a scrape."

"And scrapes get infected."

"Look, you've already rubbed it raw. There can't be a germ left."

He nudged her into the bathroom. "We'll make sure."

Before she could stop him, he took out a bottle and dumped medicine over her knuckles. What had been a dull sting turned to fire. "Damn it!"

"Here." He grabbed her hand again and began to blow on the wound. "Just give it a minute."

"A lot of good that does," she muttered, but the pain cooled.

"We'll fix dinner. That'll take your mind off it."

"You're supposed to fix dinner," she reminded him.

"Right." He kissed her forehead. "I've got to run out for a minute. I'll start the grill when I get back."

"That doesn't mean I'm going to be chopping vegetables while you're gone. I'm going to take a bath."

"Fine. If the water's still hot when I get back, I'll join you."

She didn't ask where he was going. She wanted to, but there were rules. Instead A.J. walked into the bedroom and watched from the window as he pulled out of the drive. Weary, she sat on the bed and pulled off her boots. The afternoon had taken its toll, physically, emotionally. She didn't want to think. She didn't want to feel.

Giving in, she stretched out across the bed. She'd rest for a minute, she told herself. Only for a minute.

David came home with a handful of asters he'd begged from a neighbor's garden. He thought the idea of dropping them on A.J. while she soaked in the tub might bring the laughter back to her eyes. He'd never heard her laugh so much or so easily as she had over the weekend. It wasn't something he wanted to lose. Just as he was discovering she wasn't something he wanted to lose.

He went up the stairs quietly, then paused at the bedroom door when he saw her. She'd taken off only her boots.

A pillow was crumpled under her arm as she lay diagonally across the bed. It occurred to him as he stepped into the room that he'd never watched her sleep before. They'd never given each other the chance.

Her face looked so soft, so fragile. Her hair was pale and tumbled onto her cheek, her lips unpainted and just parted. How was it he'd never noticed how delicate her features were, how slender and frail her wrists were, how elegantly feminine the curve of her neck was?

Maybe he hadn't looked, David admitted as he crossed to the bed. But he was looking now.

She was fire and thunder in bed, sharp and tough out of it. She had a gift, a curse and ability she fought against every waking moment, one that he was just beginning to understand. He was just beginning to see that it made her defensive and defenseless.

Only rarely did the vulnerabilities emerge, and then with such reluctance from her he'd tended to gloss over them. But now, just now, when she was asleep and unaware of him, she looked like something a man should protect, cherish.

The first stirrings weren't of passion and desire, but of a quiet affection he hadn't realized he felt for her. He hadn't realized it was possible to feel anything quiet for Aurora. Unable to resist, he reached down to brush the hair from her cheek and feel the warm, smooth skin beneath.

She stirred. He'd wanted her to. Heavy and sleep-glazed, her eyes opened. "David?" Even her voice was soft, feminine.

"I brought you a present." He sat on the bed beside her and dropped the flowers by her hand.

"Oh." He'd seen that before, too, he realized. That quick surprise and momentary confusion when he'd done something foolish or romantic. "You didn't have to."

"I think I did," he murmured, half to himself. Almost as an experiment, he lowered his mouth to hers and kissed her softly, gently, with the tenderness she'd made him feel as she slept. He felt the ache move through him, sweet as a dream.

"David?" She said his name again, but this time her eyes were dark and dazed.

"Ssh." His hands didn't drag through her hair now with trembles of passion, but stroked, exploring the texture. He could watch the light strike individual strands. "Lovely." He brought his gaze back to hers. "Have I ever told you how lovely you are?"

She started to reach for him, for the passion that she could understand. "It isn't necessary."

His lips met hers again, but they didn't devour and demand. This mood was foreign and made her heart pound as much with uncertainty as need. "Make love with me," she murmured as she tried to draw him down.

"I am." His mouth lingered over hers. "Maybe for the first time."

"I don't understand," she began, but he shifted so that he could cradle her in his arms.

"Neither do I."

So he began, slowly, gently, testing them both. Her mouth offered darker promises, but he waited, coaxing. His lips were patient as they moved over hers, light and soothing as they kissed her eyes closed. He didn't touch her, not yet, though he wondered what it would be like to stroke her while the light was softening, to caress as though it were all new, all fresh. Gradually he felt the tension in her body give way, he felt what he'd never felt from her before. Pliancy, surrender, warmth.

Her body seemed weightless, gloriously light and free. She felt the pleasure move through her, but sweetly, fluidly, like wine. Then he was the wine, heady and potent, drugging her with the intoxicating taste of his mouth. The hands that had clutched him in demand went lax. There was so much to absorb—the flavor of his lips as they lingered on hers; the texture of his skin as his cheek brushed hers; the scent that clung to him, part man, part woods; the dark, curious look in his eyes as he watched her.

She looked as she had when she'd slept, he thought. Fragile, so arousingly fragile. And she felt... At last he touched, fingertips only along skin already warm. He heard her sigh his name in a way she'd never said it before. Keeping her cradled in his arms, he began to take her deeper, take himself deeper, with tenderness.

She had no strength to demand, no will to take control. For the first time her body was totally his, just as for the first time her emotions were. He touched, and she yielded. He tasted, and she gave. When he shifted her, she felt as though she could float. Perhaps she was. Clouds of pleasure, mists of soft, soft delight. When he began to undress her, she opened her eyes, needing to see him again.

The light had gone to rose with sunset. It made her skin glow as he slowly drew off her shirt. He couldn't take his eyes off her, couldn't stop his hands from touching, though he had no desire to be quick. When she reached up, he helped her pull off his own shirt, then took her injured hand to his lips. He kissed her fingers, then her palm, then her wrist, until he felt her begin to tremble. Bending, he brushed her lips with his again, wanting to hear her sigh his name. Then, watching her, waiting until she looked at him, he continued to undress her.

Slowly. Achingly slowly, he drew the jeans down her legs, pausing now and then to taste newly exposed skin. Pulses beat at the back of her knees. He felt them, lingered there, exploited them. Her ankles were slim, fragile like her wrists. He traced them with his tongue until she moaned. Then he waited, letting her settle again as he stripped off his own jeans. He came to her, flesh against flesh.

Nothing had been like this. Nothing could be like this. The thoughts whirled in her brain as he began another deliciously slow assault. Her body was to be enjoyed and pleasured, not worshipped. But he did so now, and enticed her to do the same with his.

So strong. She'd known his strength before, but this was different. His fingers didn't grip; his hands didn't press. They skimmed, they traced, they weakened. So intense. They'd shared intensity before, but never so quietly.

She heard him say her name. Aurora. It was like a dream, one she'd never dared to have. He murmured promises in her ear and she believed them. Whatever tomorrow might bring she believed them now. She could smell the flowers strewn over the bed and taste the excitement that built in a way it had never done before.

He slipped into her as though their bodies had never been apart. The rhythm was easy, patient, giving.

Holding himself back, he watched her climb higher. That was what he wanted, he realized, to give her everything there was to give. When she arched and shuddered, the force whipped through him. Power, he recognized it, but was driven to leash it. His mouth found hers and drew on the sweetness. How could he have known sweetness could be so arousing?

The blood was pounding in his head, roaring in his ears, yet his body continued to move slowly with hers. Balanced on the edge, David said her name a last time.

"Aurora, look at me." When her eyes opened, they were dark and aware. "I want to see where I take you."

Even when control slipped away, echoes of tenderness remained.

Chapter Ten

Alice Robbins had exploded onto the screen in the sixties, a young, raw talent. She had, as so many girls before her and after her, fled to Hollywood to escape the limitations of small-town life. She'd come with dreams, with hopes and ambitions. An astrologer might have said Alice's stars were in the right quadrant. When she hit, she hit big.

She had had an early, turbulent marriage that had ended in an early, turbulent divorce. Scenes in and out of the courtroom had been as splashy as anything she'd portrayed on the screen. With her marriage over and her career climbing, she'd enjoyed all the benefits of being a beautiful woman in a town that demanded, then courted, beauty. Reports of her love affairs sizzled on the pages of glossies. Glowing reviews and critical praise heaped higher with each role. But in her late twenties, when her career was reaching its peak, she found something that fulfilled her in a way success and reviews never had. Alice Robbins met Peter Van Camp.

He'd been nearly twenty years her senior, a hard-bitten, well-to-do business magnate. They'd married after a whirlwind two-week courtship that had kept the gossip columns salivating. Was it for money? Was it for power? Was it for prestige? It had been, very simply, for love.

In an unprecedented move, Alice had taken her husband's name professionally as well as privately. Hardly more than a year later, she'd given birth to a son and had, without a backward glance, put her career on hold. For nearly a decade, she'd devoted herself to her family with the same kind of single-minded drive she'd put into her acting.

When word leaked that Alice Van Camp had been lured back into films, the hype had been extravagant. Rumors of a multimillion-dollar deal flew and promises of the movie of the century were lavish.

Four weeks before the release of the film, her son, Matthew, had been kidnapped.

David knew the background. Alice Van Camp's triumphs and trials were public fodder. Her name was legend. Though she rarely consented to grace the screen, her popularity remained constant. As to the abduction and recovery of her son, details were sketchy. Perhaps because of the circumstances, the police had never been fully open and Clarissa DeBasse had been quietly evasive. Neither Alice nor Peter Van Camp had ever, until now, granted an interview on the subject. Even with their agreement and apparent cooperation, David knew he would have to tread carefully.

He was using the minimum crew, and a well-seasoned one. "Star" might be an overused term, but David was aware they would be dealing with a woman who fully deserved the title and the mystique that went with it.

Her Beverly Hills home was guarded by electric gates and a wall twice as tall as a man. Just inside the gates was a uniformed guard who verified their identification. Even after they had been passed through, they drove another half a mile to the house.

It was white, flowing out with balconies, rising up with Doric columns, softened by tall, tall trellises of roses in full bloom. Legend had it that her husband had had it built for her in honor of the last role she'd played before the birth of their son. David had seen the movie countless times and remembered her as an antebellum tease who made Scarlett O'Hara look like a nun.

There were Japanese cherry trees dripping down to sweep the lawn in long skirts. Their scent and the citrus fragrance of orange and lemon stung the air. As he pulled his car to a halt behind the equipment van, he spotted a peacock strutting across the lawn.

I wish A.J. could see this.

The thought came automatically before he had time to check it, just as thoughts of her had come automatically for days. Because he wasn't yet sure just how he felt about it, David simply let it happen.

And how did he feel about her? That was something else he wasn't quite sure of. Desire. He desired her more, even more now after he'd saturated himself with her. Friendship. In some odd, cautious way he felt they were almost as much friends as they were lovers. Understanding. It was more difficult to be as definite about that. A.J. had an uncanny ability to throw up mirrors that reflected back your own thoughts rather than hers. Still, he had come to understand that beneath the confidence and drive was a warm, vulnerable woman.

She was passionate. She was reserved. She was competent. She was fragile. And she was, David had discovered, a tantalizing mystery to be solved, one layer at a time.

Perhaps that was why he'd found himself so caught up in her. Most of the women he knew were precisely what they seemed. Sophisticated. Ambitious. Well-bred. His own taste had invariably drawn him to a certain type of woman. A.J. fit. Aurora didn't. If he understood anything about her, he understood she was both.

As an agent, he knew she was pleased with the deal she'd made for her client, including the Van Camp segment. As a daughter, he sensed she was uneasy about the repercussions.

But the deal had been made, David reminded himself as he walked up the wide circular steps to the Van Camp estate. As a producer, he was satisfied with the progress of his project. But as a man, he wished he knew of a way to put A.J.'s mind at rest. She excited him; she intrigued him. And as no woman had ever done before, she concerned him. He'd wondered, more often than once, if that peculiar combination equaled love. And if it did, what in hell he was going to do about it.

"Second thoughts?" Alex asked as David hesitated at the door.

Annoyed with himself, David shrugged his shoulders, then pushed the bell. "Should there be?"

"Clarissa's comfortable with this."

David found himself shifting restlessly. "That's enough for you?"

"It's enough," Alex answered. "Clarissa knows her own mind."

The phrasing had him frowning, had him searching. "Alex—"

Though he wasn't certain what he had been about to say, the door opened and the moment was lost. A formally dressed, French-accented maid took their names before leading them into a room off the main hall. The crew, not easily impressed, spoke in murmurs.

It was unapologetically Hollywood. The furnishings were big and bold, the colors flashy. On a baby grand in the center of the room was a silver candelabra dripping with crystal prisms. David recognized it as a prop from *Music at Midnight*.

"Not one for understatements," Alex commented.

"No." David took another sweep of the room. There were brocades and silks in jewel colors. Furniture gleamed like mirrors. "But Alice Van Camp might be one of the few in the business who deserves to bang her own drum."

"Thank you."

Regal, amused and as stunning as she had been in her screen debut, Alice Van Camp paused in the doorway. She was a woman who knew how to pose, and who did so without a second thought. Like others who had known her only through her movies, David's first thought was how small she was. Then she stepped forward and her presence alone whisked the image away.

"Mr. Marshall." Hand extended, Alice walked to him. Her hair was a deep sable spiked around a face as pale and smooth as a child's. If he hadn't known better, David would have said she'd yet to see thirty. "It's a pleasure to meet you. I'm a great admirer of journalists—when they don't misquote me."

"Mrs. Van Camp." He covered her small hand with both of his. "Shall I say the obvious?"

"That depends."

"You're just as beautiful face to face as you are on the screen."

She laughed, the smoky, sultry murmur that had made men itch for more than two decades. "I appreciate the obvious. And you're David Brady." Her gaze shifted to him and he felt the unapologetic summing up, strictly woman to man. "I've seen several of your productions. My husband prefers documentaries and biographies to films. I can't think why he married me."

"I can." David accepted her hand. "I'm an avid fan."

"As long as you don't tell me you've enjoyed my movies since you were a child." Amusement glimmered in her eyes again before she glanced around. "Now if you'll introduce me to our crew, we can get started."

David had admired her for years. After ten minutes in her company, his admiration grew. She spoke to each member of the crew, from the director down to the assistant lighting technician. When she'd finished, she turned herself over to Sam for instructions.

At her suggestion, they moved to the terrace. Patient, she waited while technicians set up reflectors and umbrellas to exploit the best effect from available light. Her maid set a table of cold drinks and snacks out of camera range. Though she didn't touch a thing, she indicated to the crew that they should enjoy. She sat easily through sound tests and blocking. When Sam was satisfied, she turned to Alex and began.

"Mrs. Van Camp, for twenty years you've been known as one of the most talented and best-loved actresses in the country."

"Thank you, Alex. My career has always been one of the most important parts of my life."

"One of the most. We're here now to discuss another part of your life. Your family, most specifically your son. A decade ago, you nearly faced tragedy."

"Yes, I did." She folded her hands. Though the sun shone down in her face, she never blinked. "A tragedy that I sincerely doubt I would have recovered from."

"This is the first interview you've given on this subject. Can I ask you why you agreed now?"

She smiled a little, leaning back in her weathered rattan chair. "Timing, in life and in business, is crucial. For several years after my son's abduction I simply couldn't speak of it. After a time, it seemed unnecessary to bring it up again. Now, if I watch the news or look in a store window and see posters of missing children, I ache for the parents."

"Do you consider that this interview might help those parents?"

"Help them find their children, no." Emotion flickered in her eyes, very real and very brief. "But perhaps it can ease some of the misery. I'd never considered sharing my feelings about my own experience. And I doubt very much if I would have agreed if it hadn't been for Clarissa DeBasse."

"Clarissa DeBasse asked you to give this interview?"

After a soft laugh, Alice shook her head. "Clarissa never asks anything. But when I spoke with her and I realized she had faith in this project, I agreed."

"You have a great deal of faith in her."

"She gave me back my son."

She said it with such simplicity, with such utter sincerity, that Alex let the sentence hang. From somewhere in the garden at her back, a bird began to trill.

"That's what we'd like to talk about here. Will you tell us how you came to know Clarissa DeBasse?"

Behind the cameras, behind the crew, David stood with his hands in his pockets and listened to the story. He remembered how A.J. had once told him of her mother's gradual association with celebrities. Alice Van Camp had come to her with a friend on a whim. After an hour, she'd gone away impressed with Clarissa's gentle style and straightforward manner. On impulse, she'd commissioned Clarissa to do her husband's chart as a gift for their anniversary. When it was done, even the pragmatic and business-oriented Peter Van Camp had been intrigued.

"She told me things about myself," Alice went on. "Not about tomorrow, you understand, but about my feelings, things about my background that had influenced me, or still worried me. I can't say I always liked what she had to say. There are things about ourselves we don't like to admit. But I kept going back because she was so intriguing, and gradually we became friends."

"You believed in clairvoyance?"

Alice's brows drew together as she considered. "I would say I first began to see her because it was fun, it was different. I'd chosen to lead a secluded life after the birth of my son, but that didn't mean I wouldn't appreciate, even need, little touches of flash. Of the unique." The frown smoothed as she smiled. "Clarissa was undoubtedly unique."

"So you went to her for entertainment."

"Oh, yes, that was definitely the motivation in the beginning. You see, at first I thought she was simply very clever. Then, as I began to know her, I discovered she was not simply clever, she was special. That certainly doesn't mean I endorse every palmist on Sunset Boulevard. I certainly can't claim to understand the testing and research that's done on the subject. I do believe, however, that there are some of us who are more sensitive, or whose senses are more finely tuned."

"Will you tell us what happened when your son was abducted?"

"June 22. Almost ten years ago." Alice closed her eyes a moment. "To me it's yesterday. You have children, Mr. Marshall?"

"Yes, I do."

"And you love them."

"Very much."

"Then you have some small glimmer of what it would be like to lose them, even for a short time. There's terror and there's guilt. The guilt is nearly as painful as the fear. You see, I hadn't been with him when he'd been taken. Jenny was Matthew's nanny. She'd been with us over five years and was very devoted to my son. She was young, but dependable and fiercely protective. When I made the decision to go back into films, we leaned on Jenny heavily. Neither my husband nor myself wanted Matthew to suffer because I was working again."

"Your son was nearly ten when you agreed to do another movie."

"Yes, he was quite independent already. Both Peter and I wanted that for him. Very often during the filming, Jenny would bring him to the studio. Even after the shooting was complete, she continued in her habit of walking to the park with him in the afternoon. If I had realized then how certain habits can be dangerous, I would have stopped it. Both my husband and myself had been careful to keep Matthew out of the limelight, not because we were afraid for him physically, but because we felt it was best that his upbringing be as normal and natural as possible. Of course he was recognized, and now and then some enterprising photographer would get a shot in."

"Did that sort of thing bother you?"

"No." When she smiled, the sultry glamour came through. "I suppose I was accustomed to such things. Peter and I didn't want to be fanatics about our privacy. And I wonder, and always have, if we'd been stricter would it have made any difference? I doubt it." There was a little sigh, as though it were a point she'd yet to resolve. "We learned later that Matthew's visits to the park were being watched."

"For a time the police suspected Jennifer Waite, your son's nanny, of working with the kidnappers."

"That was, of course, absurd. I never for a minute doubted Jenny's loyalty and devotion to Matthew. Once it was over, she was completely cleared." A trace of stubbornness came through. "She's still in my employ."

"The investigators found her story disjointed."

"The afternoon he was abducted, Jenny came home hysterical. We were the closest thing to family she had, and she blamed herself. Matthew had been playing ball with several other children while she watched. A young woman had come up to her asking for directions. She'd spun a story about missing her bus and being new in town. She'd distracted Jenny only a few moments, and that's all it took. When she looked back, Jenny saw Matthew being hustled into a car at the edge of the park. She ran after him, but he was gone. Ten minutes after she came home alone the first ransom call came in."

She lifted her hands to her lips a moment, and they trembled lightly. "I'm sorry. Could we stop here a moment?"

"Cut. Five minutes," Sam ordered the crew.

David was beside her chair before Sam had finished speaking. "Would you like something, Mrs. Van Camp? A drink?"

"No." She shook her head and looked beyond him. "It isn't as easy as I thought it would be. Ten years, and it still isn't easy."

"I could send for your husband."

"I told Peter to stay away today because he's always so uncomfortable around cameras. I wish I hadn't."

"We can wrap for today."

"Oh, no." She took a deep breath and composed herself. "I believe in finishing what I start. Matthew's a sophomore in college." She smiled up at David. "Do you like happy endings?"

He held her hand. For the moment she was only a woman. "I'm a sucker for them."

"He's bright, handsome and in love. I just needed to remember that. It could have been..." She linked her hands again and the ruby on her finger shone like blood. "It could have been much different. You know Clarissa's daughter, don't you?"

A bit off-balance at the change of subject, David shifted. "Yes."

She admired the caution. "I meant it when I said Clarissa and I are friends. Mothers worry about their children. Do you have a cigarette?"

In silence he took one out and lit it for her.

Alice blew out smoke and let some of the tension fade. "She's a hell of an agent. Do you know, I wanted to sign with her and she wouldn't have me?"

David forgot his own cigarette in simple astonishment. "I beg your pardon?"

Alice laughed again and relaxed. She'd needed a moment to remember life went on. "It was a few months after

the kidnapping. A.J. figured I'd come to her out of gratitude to Clarissa. And maybe I had. In any case, she turned
me down flat, even though she was scrambling around trying to rent decent office space. I admired her integrity. So
much so that a few years ago I approached her again." Alice smiled at him, enjoying the fact that he listened very
carefully. Apparently, she mused, Clarissa was right on tar-
get, as always. "She was established, respected. And she
turned me down again."

What agent in her right mind would turn down a top
name, a name that had earned through sheer talent the label of "megastar"? "A.J. never quite does what you expect," he murmured.

"Clarissa's daughter is a woman who insists on being accepted for herself, but can't always tell when she is." She
crushed out the cigarette after a second quick puff.
"Thanks. I'd like to continue now."

Within moments, Alice was deep into her own story.
Though the camera continued to roll, she forgot about it.
Sitting in the sunlight with the scent of roses strong and
sweet, she talked about her hours of terror.

"We would have paid anything. Anything. Peter and I
fought bitterly about calling in the police. The kidnappers
had been very specific. We weren't to contact anyone. But
Peter felt, and rightly so, that we needed help. The ransom
calls came every few hours. We agreed to pay, but they kept
changing the terms. Testing us. It was the worst kind of
cruelty. While we waited, the police began searching for the
car Jenny had seen and the woman she'd spoken with in the
park. It was as if they'd vanished into thin air. At the end of
forty-eight hours, we were no closer to finding Matthew."

"So you decided to call in Clarissa DeBasse?"

"I don't know when the idea of asking Clarissa to help
came to me. I know I hadn't slept or eaten. I just kept waiting for the phone to ring. It's such a helpless feeling. I re-

membered, God knows why, that Clarissa had once told me where to find a diamond brooch I'd misplaced. It wasn't just a piece of jewelry to me, but something Peter had given me when Matthew was born. A child isn't a brooch, but I began to think, maybe, just maybe. I needed some hope.

"The police didn't like the idea. I don't believe Peter did, either, but he knew I needed something. I called Clarissa and I told her that Matthew had been taken." Her eyes filled. She didn't bother to blink the tears away. "I asked her if she could help me and she told me she'd try.

"I broke down when she arrived. She sat with me awhile, friend to friend, mother to mother. She spoke to Jenny, though there was no calming the poor girl down even at that point. The police were very terse with Clarissa, but she seemed to accept that. She told them they were looking in the wrong place." Unself-consciously she brushed at the tears on her cheek. "I can tell you that didn't sit too well with the men who'd been working around the clock. She told them Matthew hadn't been taken out of the city, he hadn't gone north as they'd thought. She asked for something of Matthew's, something he would have worn. I brought her the pajamas he'd worn to bed the night before. They were blue with little cars across the top. She just sat there, running them through her hands. I remember wanting to scream at her, plead with her, to give me something. Then she started to speak very quietly.

"Matthew was only miles away, she said. He hadn't been taken into San Francisco, though the police had traced one of the ransom calls there. She said he was still in Los Angeles. She described the street, then the house. A white house with blue shutters on a corner lot. I'll never forget the way she described the room in which he was being held. It was dark, you see, and Matthew, though he always tried to be brave, was still afraid of the dark. She said there were only two people in the house, one man and the woman who had spoken to Jenny in the park. She thought there was a car in the drive, gray or green, she said. And she told me he wasn't hurt. He was afraid—'' her voice shuddered, then strengthened ''—but he wasn't hurt.''

"And the police pursued the lead?"

"They didn't have much faith in it, naturally enough, but they sent out cars to look for the house she'd described. I don't know who was more stunned when they found it, Peter and myself or the police. They got Matthew out without a struggle because the two kidnappers with him weren't expecting any trouble. The third accomplice was in San Fransico, making all the calls. The police also found the car he'd been abducted in there.

"Clarissa stayed until Matthew was home, until he was safe. Later he told me about the room he'd been held in. It was exactly as she'd described it."

"Mrs. Van Camp, a lot of people claimed that the abduction and the dramatic rescue of your son was a publicity stunt to hype the release of your first movie since his birth."

"That didn't matter to me." With only her voice, with only her eyes, she showed her complete contempt. "They could say and believe whatever they wanted. I had my son back."

"And you believe Clarissa DeBasse is responsible for that?"

"I know she is."

"Cut," Sam mumbled to his cameraman before he walked to Alice. "Mrs. Van Camp, if we can get a few reaction shots and over the shoulder angles, we'll be done."

He could go now. David knew there was no real reason for him to remain during the angle changes. The shoot was essentially finished, and had been everything he could have asked for. Alice Van Camp was a consummate actress, but no one watching this segment would consider that she played a part. She'd been a mother, reliving an experience every mother fears. And she had, by the telling, brought the core of his project right back to Clarissa.

He thought perhaps he understood a little better why A.J. had had mixed feelings about the interview. Alice Van Camp had suffered in the telling. If his instincts were right, Clarissa would have suffered, too. It seemed to him that empathy was an intimate part of her gift.

Nevertheless he stayed behind the camera and restlessly waited until the shoot was complete. Though he detected a trace of weariness in her eyes, Alice escorted the crew to the door herself.

"A remarkable woman," Alex commented as they walked down the circular steps toward the drive.

"And then some. But you've got one yourself."

"I certainly do." Alex pulled out the cigar he'd been patiently waiting for for more than three hours. "I might be a little biased, but I believe you have one, as well."

Frowning, David paused by his car. "I haven't got A.J." It occurred to him that it was the first time he had thought of it in precisely those terms.

"Clarissa seems to think you do."

He turned back and leaned against his car. "And approves?"

"Shouldn't she?"

He pulled out a cigarette. The restlessness was growing. "I don't know."

"You were going to ask me something earlier, before we went in. Do you want to ask me now?"

It had been nagging at him. David wondered if by stating it aloud it would ease. "Clarissa isn't an ordinary woman. Does it bother you?"

Alex took a contented puff on his cigar. "It certainly intrigues me, and I'd be lying if I didn't admit I've had one or two uneasy moments. What I feel for her cancels out the fact

that I have five senses and she has what we might call six.
You're having uneasy moments." He smiled a little when
David said nothing. "Clarissa doesn't believe in keeping
secrets. We've talked about her daughter."

"I'm not sure A.J. would be comfortable with that."

"No, maybe not. It's more to the point what you're
comfortable with. You know the trouble with a man your
age, David? You consider yourself too old to go take foolish risks and too young to trust impulse. I thank God I'm
not thirty." With a smile, he walked over to hitch a ride back
to town with Sam.

He was too old to take foolish risks, David thought as he
pulled his door open. And a man who trusted impulse usually landed flat on his face. But he wanted to see her. He
wanted to see her now.

A.J.'s briefcase weighed heavily as she pulled it from the
front seat. Late rush-hour traffic streamed by the front of
her building. If she'd been able to accomplish more during
office hours, she reminded herself as she lugged up her case,
she wouldn't have to plow through papers tonight. She
would have accomplished more if she hadn't been uneasy,
thinking of the Van Camp interview.

It was over now, she told herself as she turned the key to
lock both car doors. The filming of the documentary was all
but over. She had other clients, other projects, other contracts. It was time she put her mind on them. Shifting her
briefcase to her free hand, she turned and collided with David.

"I like running into you," he murmured as he slid his
hands up her hips.

She'd had the wind knocked out of her. That's what she
told herself as she struggled for breath and leaned into him.
After a man and a woman had been intimate, after they'd
been lovers, they didn't feel breathless and giddy when they

saw each other. But she found herself wanting to wrap her arms around him and laugh.

"You might have cracked a rib," she told him, and contented herself with smiling up at him. "I certainly didn't expect to see you around this evening."

"Problem?"

"No." She let herself brush a hand through his hair. "I think I can work you in. How did the shoot go?"

He heard it, the barest trace of nerves. Not tonight, he told himself. There would be no nerves tonight. "It's done. You know, I like the way you smell up close." He lowered his mouth to brush it over her throat. "Up very close."

"David, we're standing in the parking lot."

"Mmm-hmm." He shifted his mouth to her ear and sent the thrill tumbling to her toes.

"David." She turned her head to ward him off and found her mouth captured by his in a long, lingering kiss.

"I can't stop thinking about you," he murmured, then kissed her again, hard, until the breath was trembling from her mouth into his. "I can't get you out of my mind. Sometimes I wonder if you've put a spell on me. Mind over matter."

"Don't talk. Come inside with me."

"We don't talk enough." He put his hand under her chin and drew her away before he gave in and buried himself in her again. "Sooner or later we're going to have to."

That's what she was afraid of. When they talked, really talked, she was sure it would be about the end. "Later, then. Please." She rested her cheek against his. "For now let's just enjoy each other."

He felt the edge of frustration compete with the first flares of desire. "That's all you want?"

No, no, she wanted more, everything, anything. If she opened her mouth to speak of one wish, she would speak of dozens. "It's enough," she said almost desperately. "Why did you come here tonight?"

"Because I wanted you. Because I damn well can't keep away from you."

"And that's all I need." Was she trying to convince him or herself? Neither of them had the answer. "Come inside, I'll show you."

Because he needed, because he wasn't yet sure of the nature of his own needs, he took her hand in his and went with her.

Chapter Eleven

"Are you sure you want to do this?" A.J. felt it was only fair to give David one last chance before he committed himself.

"I'm sure."

"It's going to take the better part of your evening."

"Want to get rid of me?"

"No." She smiled but still hesitated. "Ever done anything like this before?"

He took the collar of her blouse between his thumb and forefinger and rubbed. The practical A.J. had a weakness for silk. "You're my first."

"Then you'll have to do what you're told."

He skimmed his finger down her throat. "Don't you trust me?"

She cocked her head and gave him a long look. "I haven't decided. But under the circumstances, I'll take a chance. Pull up a chair." She indicated the table behind her. There were stacks of paper, neatly arranged. A.J. picked up a pencil, freshly sharpened, and handed it to him. "The first thing you can do is mark off the names I give you. Those are the people who've sent an acceptance. I'll give you the name and the number of people under that name. I need an amount for the caterer by the end of the week."

"Sounds easy enough."

"Just shows you've never dealt with a caterer," A.J. mumbled, and took her own chair.

"What's this?" As he reached for another pile of papers, she waved his hand away.

"People who've already sent gifts, and don't mess with the system. When we finish with this, we have to deal with the guests coming in from out of town. I'm hoping to book a block of rooms tomorrow."

He studied the tidy but extensive arrangement of papers spread between them. "I thought this was supposed to be a small, simple wedding."

She sent him a mild look. "There's no such thing as a small, simple wedding. I've spent two full mornings haggling with florists and over a week off and on struggling with caterers."

"Learn anything?"

"Elopement is the wisest course. Now here—"

"Would you?"

"Would I what?"

"Elope."

With a laugh, A.J. picked up her first stack of papers. "If I ever lost a grip on myself and decided on marriage, I think I'd fly to Vegas, swing through one of those drive-in chapels and have it over with."

His eyes narrowed as he listened to her, as if he were trying to see beyond the words. "Not very romantic."

"Neither am I."

"Aren't you?" He put a hand over hers, surprising her. There was something proprietary in the gesture, and something completely natural.

"No." But her fingers linked with his. "There's not a lot of room for romance in business."

"And otherwise?"

"Otherwise romance tends to lead you to see things that aren't really there. I like illusions on the stage and screen, not in my life."

"What do you want in your life, Aurora? You've never told me."

Why was she nervous? It was foolish, but he was looking at her so closely. He was asking questions he'd never asked. And the answers weren't as simple as she'd once thought. "Success," she told him. Hadn't it always been true?

He nodded, but his thumb moved gently up and down the side of her hand. "You run a successful agency already. What else?" He was waiting, for one word, one sign. Did she need him? For the first time in his life he wanted to be needed.

"I . . ." She was fumbling for words. He seemed to be the only one who could make her fumble. What did he want? What answer would satisfy him? "I suppose I want to know I've earned my own way."

"Is that why you turned down Alice Van Camp as a client?"

"She told you that?" They hadn't discussed the Van Camp interview. A.J. had purposely talked around it for days.

"She mentioned it." She'd pulled her hand from his. David wondered why every time they talked, really talked, she seemed to draw farther away from him.

"It was kind of her to come to me when I was just getting started and things were . . . rough." She shrugged her shoulders, then began to slide her pencil through her fingers. "But it was out of gratitude to my mother. I couldn't sign my first big client out of gratitude."

"Then later you turned her down again."

"It was too personal." She fought the urge to stand up, walk away from the table, and from him.

"No mixing business with personal relationships."

"Exactly. Do you want some coffee before we get started?"

"You mixed a business and personal relationship with me."

Her fingers tightened on the pencil. He watched them. "Yes, I did."

"Why?"

Though it cost her, she kept her eyes on his. He could strip her bare, she knew. If she told him she had fallen in love with him, had started the tumble almost from the first, she would have no defense left. He would have complete and total control. And she would have reneged on the most important agreement in her life. If she couldn't give him the truth, she could give him the answer he'd understand. The answer that mirrored his feelings for her.

"Because I wanted you," she said, and kept her voice cool. "I was attracted to you, and wisely or not, I gave in to the attraction."

He felt the twinge, a need unfulfilled. "That's enough for you?"

Hadn't she said he could hurt her? He was hurting her now with every word. "Why shouldn't it be?" She gave him an easy smile and waited for the ache to pass.

"Why shouldn't it be?" he murmured, and tried to accept the answer for what it was. He pulled out a cigarette, then began carefully. "I think you should know we're shooting a segment on the Ridehour case." Though his eyes stayed on hers, he saw her tense. "Clarissa agreed to discuss it."

"She told me. That should wrap the taping?"

"It should." She was holding back. Though no more than a table separated them, it might have been a canyon. "You don't like it."

"No, I don't, but I'm trying to learn that Clarissa has to make her own decisions."

"A.J., she seems very easy about it."

"You don't understand."

"Then let me."

"Before I convinced her to move, to keep her residence strictly confidential, she had closets full of letters." She took her glasses off to rub at a tiny ache in her temple. "People asking for her to help them. Some of them involved no more than asking her to locate a ring, and others were full of problems so heartbreaking they gave you nightmares."

"She couldn't help everyone."

"That's what I kept telling her. When she moved down to Newport Beach, things eased up. Until she got the call from San Francisco."

"The Ridehour murders."

"Yes." The ache grew. "There was never a question of her listening to me on that one. I don't believe she heard one argument I made. She just packed. When I saw there was no stopping her from going, I went with her." She kept her breathing even with great effort. Her hands were steady only because she locked them so tightly together. "It was one of the most painful experiences of her life. She saw." A.J. closed her eyes and spoke to him what she'd never spoken to anyone. "I saw."

When he covered her hand with his he found it cold. He didn't have to see her eyes to know the baffled fear would be there. Comfort, understanding. How did he show them? "Why didn't you tell me before?"

She opened her eyes. The control was there but teetering. "It isn't something I like to remember. I've never before or since had anything come so clear, so hideously clear."

"We'll cut it."

She gave him a blank, puzzled look. "What?"

"We'll cut the segment."

"Why?"

Slowly he drew her hands apart and into his. He wanted to explain, to tell her so that she'd understand. He wished he had the words. "Because it upsets you. That's enough."

She looked down at their hands. His looked so strong, so dependable over hers. No one except her mother had ever offered to do anything for her without an angle. Yet it seemed he was. "I don't know what to say to you."

"Don't say anything."

"No." She gave herself a moment. For reasons she couldn't understand, she was relaxed again. Tension was there, hovering, but the knots in her stomach had eased. "Clarissa agreed to this segment, so she must feel as though it should be done."

"We're not talking about Clarissa now, but you. Aurora, I said once I never wanted to be responsible for your going through something like this. I mean it."

"I think you do." It made all the difference. "The fact that you'd cut the segment because of me makes me feel very special."

"Maybe I should have told you that you are before now."

Longings rose up. She let herself feel them for only a moment. "You don't have to tell me anything. I realize that if you cut this part because of me I'd hate myself. It was a long time ago, David. Maybe it's time I learned to deal with reality a little better."

"Maybe you deal with it too well."

"Maybe." She smiled again. "In any case I think you should do the segment. Just do a good job of it."

"I intend to. Do you want to sit in on it?"

"No." She glanced down at the stacks of papers. "Alex will be there for her."

He heard it in her voice, not doubt but resignation. "He's crazy about her."

"I know." In a lightning change of mood, she picked up her pencil again. "I'm going to give them one hell of a wedding."

He grinned at her. Resiliency was only one of the things that attracted him to her. "We'd better get started."

They worked side by side for nearly two hours. It took half that time for the tension to begin to fade. They read off lists and compiled new ones. They analyzed and calculated how many cases of champagne would be adequate and argued over whether to serve salmon mousse or iced shrimp.

She hadn't expected him to become personally involved with planning her mother's wedding. Before they'd finished, she'd come to accept it to the point where she delegated him to help seat guests at the ceremony.

"Working with you's an experience, A.J."

"Hmm?" She counted the out of town guests one last time.

"If I needed an agent, you'd head the list."

She glanced up, but was too cautious to smile. "Is that a compliment?"

"Not exactly."

Now she smiled. When she took off her glasses, her face was abruptly vulnerable. "I didn't think so. Well, once I give these figures to the caterer, that should be it. Everyone who attends will have me to thank that they aren't eating Clarissa's Swedish meatballs. And you." She set the lists aside. "I appreciate all the help."

"I'm fond of Clarissa."

"I know. I appreciate that, too. Now I think you deserve a reward." She leaned closer and caught her tongue in her teeth. "Anything in mind?"

He had plenty in mind every time he looked at her. "We can start with that coffee."

"Coming right up." She rose, and out of habit glanced at her watch. "Oh, God."

He reached for a cigarette. "Problem?"

"*Empire*'s on."

"A definite problem."

"No, I have to watch it."

As she dashed over to the television, he shook his head. "All this time, and I had no idea you were an addict. A.J., there are places you can go that can help you deal with these things."

"Ssh." She settled on the sofa, relieved she'd missed no more than the opening credits. "I have a client—"

"It figures."

"She has a lot of potential," A.J. continued. "But this is the first real break we've gotten. She's only signed for four episodes, but if she does well, they could bring her back through next season."

Resigned, he joined her on the sofa. "Aren't these repeats, anyway?"

"Not this one. It's a teaser for a spin-off that's going to run through the summer."

"A spin-off?" He propped his feet on an issue of *Variety* on the coffee table. "Isn't there enough sex and misery in one hour a week?"

"Melodrama. It's important to the average person to see that the filthy rich have their problems. See him?" Reaching over, she dug into a bowl of candied almonds. "That's Dereck, the patriarch. He made his money in shipping—and smuggling. He's determined that his children carry on his business, by his rules. That's Angelica."

"In the hot tub."

"Yes, she's his second wife. She married him for his money and power and enjoys every minute of them. But she hates his kids."

"And they hate her right back."

"That's the idea." Pleased with him, A.J. patted his leg. "Now the setup is that Angelica's illegitimate daughter from a long-ago relationship is going to show up. That's my client."

"Like mother like daughter?"

"Oh, yes, she gets to play the perfect bitch. Her name's Lavender."

"Of course it is."

"You see, Angelica never told Dereck she had a daughter, so when Lavender shows up, she's going to cause all sorts of problems. Now Beau—that's Dereck's eldest son—"

"No more names." With a sigh, he swung his arm over the back of the sofa. "I'll just watch all the skin and diamonds."

"Just because you'd rather watch pelicans migrate— Here she is."

A.J. bit her lip. She tensed, agonizing with her client over each line, each move, each expression. And she would, David thought with a smile, fluff him off if he mentioned she had a personal involvement. Just business? Not by a long shot. She was pulling for her ingenue and ten percent didn't enter into it.

"Oh, she's good," A.J. breathed at the commercial break. "She's really very good. A season—maybe two—of this, and we'll be sifting through offers for feature films."

"Her timing's excellent." He might consider the show itself a glitzy waste of time, but he appreciated talent. "Where did she study?"

"She didn't." Smug, A.J. sat back. "She took a bus from Kansas City and ended up in my reception area with a homemade portfolio and a handful of high school plays to her credit."

He gave in and tried the candied almonds himself. "You usually sign on clients that way?"

"I usually have Abe or one of the more maternal members of my staff give them a lecture and a pat on the head."

"Sensible. But?"

"She was different. When she wouldn't budge out of the office for the second day running, I decided to see her myself. As soon as I saw her I knew. Not that way," she answered, understanding his unspoken question. "I make it a policy not to sign a client no matter what feelings might come through. She had looks and a wonderful voice. But more, she had the drive. I don't know how many auditions I sent her on in the first few weeks. But I figured if she survived that, we were going to roll." She watched the next glittery set of *Empire* appear on the screen. "And we're rolling."

"It took guts to camp out in one of the top agencies in Hollywood."

"If you don't have guts in this town, you'll be flattened in six months."

"Is that what keeps you on top, A.J.?"

"It's part of it." She found the curve of his shoulder an easy place to rest her head. "You can't tell me you think you're where you are today because you got lucky."

"No. You start off thinking hard work's enough, then you realize you have to take risks and shed a little blood. Then just when everything comes together and a project's finished and successful, you have to start another and prove yourself all over again."

"It's a lousy business." A.J. cuddled against him.

"Yep."

"Why do you do it?" Forgetting the series, forgetting her client, A.J. turned her head to look at him.

"Masochism."

"No, really."

"Because every time I watch something I did on that little screen, it's like Christmas. And I get every present I ever wanted."

"I know." Nothing he could have said could have hit more directly home. "I attended the Oscars a couple of years ago and two of my clients won. Two of them." She let her eyes close as she leaned against him. "I sat in the audience watching, and it was the biggest thrill of my life. I know some people would say you're not asking for enough when you get your thrills vicariously, but it's enough, more than enough, to know you've had a part in something like that. Maybe your name isn't a household world, but you were the catalyst.''

"Not everyone wants his name to be a household word.''

"Yours could be.'' She shifted again to look at him. "I'm not just saying that because—'' *Because I love you.* The phrase was nearly out before she checked it. When he lifted his brow at her sudden silence, she continued quickly. "Because of our relationship. With the right material, the right crew, you could be one of the top ten producers in the business.''

"I appreciate that.'' Her eyes were so earnest, so intense. He wished he knew why. "I don't think you throw around compliments without thinking about them first.''

"No, I don't. I've seen your work, and I've seen the way you work. And I've been around long enough to know.''

"I don't have any desire, not at this point, anyway, to tie myself up with any of the major studios. The big screen's for fantasies.'' He touched her cheek. It was real; it was soft. "I prefer dealing in reality.''

"So produce something real.'' It was a challenge—she knew it. By the look in his eyes he knew it, as well.

"Such as?''

"I have a script.''

"A.J.—''

"No hear me out. David.'' She said his name in frustration when he rolled her under him on the sofa. "Just listen a minute.''

"I'd rather bite your ear.''

"Bite it all you want. After you listen.''

"Negotiations again?'' He drew himself up just to look down at her. Her eyes were lit with enthusiasm, her cheeks flushed with anticipation of excitement to come. "What script?" he asked, and watched her lips curve.

"I've done some business with George Steiger. You know him?"

"We've met. He's an excellent writer."

"He's written a screenplay. His first. It just happened to come across my desk."

"Just happened?"

She'd done him a few favors. He was asking for another. Doing favors without personal gain at the end didn't fit the image she'd worked hard on developing. "We don't need to get into that. It's wonderful, David, really wonderful. It deals with the Cherokees and what they called the Trail of Tears, when they were driven from Georgia to reservations in Oklahoma. Most of the point of view is through a small child. You sense the bewilderment, the betrayal, but there's this strong thread of hope. It's not your 'ride off into the sunset' Western and it's not a pretty story. It's real. You could make it important."

She was selling, and doing a damn good job of it. It occurred to him she'd probably never pitched a deal while curled up on the sofa before. "A.J., what makes you think that if I were interested, Steiger would be interested in me?"

"I happened to mention that I knew you."

"Happened to again?"

"Yes." She smiled and ran her hands down to his hips. "He's seen your work and knows your reputation. David, he needs a producer, the right producer."

"And so?"

As if disinterested, she skimmed her fingertips up his back. "He asked if I'd mention it to you, all very informally."

"This is definitely informal," he murmured as he fit his body against hers. "Are you playing agent, A.J.?"

"No." Her eyes were abruptly serious as she took his face in her hands. "I'm being your friend."

She touched him, more deeply, more sweetly than any of their loving, any of their passion. For a moment he could find nothing to say. "Every time I think I've got a track on you, you switch lanes."

"Will you read it?"

He kissed one cheek, then the other, in a gesture he'd seen her use with her mother. It meant affection, devotion. He wondered if she understood. "I guess that means you can get me a copy."

"I just happened to have brought one home with me." With a laugh, she threw her arms around him. "David, you're going to love it."

"I'd rather love you."

She stiffened, but only for a heartbeat. Their loving was physical, she reminded herself. Deeply satisfying but only physical. When he spoke of love, it didn't mean the emotions, but the body. It was all she could expect from him, and all he wanted from her.

"Then love me now," she murmured, and found his mouth with hers. "Love me now."

She drew him to her, tempting him to take everything at once, quickly, heatedly. But he learned that pleasure taken slowly, given gently, could be so much more gratifying. Because it was still so new, she responded to tenderness with hesitation. Her stomach fluttered when he skimmed her lips with his, offering, promising. She heard her own sigh escape, a soft, giving sound that whispered across his lips. Then he murmured her name, quietly, as if it were the only sound he needed to hear.

No rush. His needs seemed to meld with her own. No hurry. Content, she let herself enjoy easy kisses that aroused the soul before they tempted the body. Relaxed, she allowed herself to thrill to the light caresses that made her strong enough to accept being weak.

She wanted to feel him against her without boundaries. With a murmur of approval, she pulled his shirt over his head, then took her hands on a long stroke down his back. There was the strength she'd understood from the beginning. A strength she respected, perhaps even more now that his hands were gentle.

When had she looked for gentleness? Her mind was already too clouded to know if she ever had. But now that she'd found it, she never wanted to lose it. Or him.

"I want you, David." She whispered the words along his cheek as she drew him closer.

Hearing her say it made his heart pound. He'd heard the words before, but rarely from her and never with such quiet acceptance. He lifted his head to look down at her. "Tell me again." As he took her chin in his hand, his voice was low and husky with emotion. "Tell me again, when I'm looking at you."

"I want you."

His mouth crushed down on hers, smothering any more words, any more thoughts. He seemed to need more; she thought she could feel it, though she didn't know what to give. She offered her mouth, that his might hungrily meet it. She offered her body, that his could greedily take it. But she held back her heart, afraid he would take that, as well, and damage it.

Clothes were peeled off as patience grew thin. He wanted to feel her against him, all the long length of her. He trembled when he touched her, but he was nearly used to trembling for her now. He ached, as he always ached. Light and subtle along her skin was the path of scent. He could follow it from her throat, to the hollow of her breasts, to the pulse at the inside of her elbows.

She shuddered against him. Her body seemed to pulse, then sigh, with each touch, each stroke. He knew where the brush of a fingertip would arouse, or the nip of his teeth would inflame. And she knew his body as intimately. Her lips would find each point of pleasure; her palms would stroke each flame higher.

He grew to need. Each time he loved her he came to need not only what she would give, but what she could. Each time he was more desperate to draw more from her, knowing that if he didn't find the key, he'd beg. She could, simply because she asked for nothing, bring him to his knees.

"Tell me what you want," he demanded as she clung to him.

"You. I want you."

She was hovering above the clouds that shook with lightning and thunder. The air was thick and heavy, the heat swirling. Her body was his; she gave it willingly. But the heart she struggled so hard to defend lost itself to him.

"David." All the love, all the emotion she felt, shimmered in his name as she pressed herself against him. "Don't let me go."

They dozed, still wrapped together, still drowsily content. Though most of his weight was on her, she felt light, free. Each time they made love, the sense of her own freedom came stronger. She was bound to him, but more liberated than she had ever been in her life. So she lay quietly as his heart beat slowly and steadily against hers.

"TV's still on," David murmured.

"Um-hmm." The late night movie whisked by, sirens blaring, guns blasting. She didn't care.

She linked her hands behind his waist. "Doesn't matter."

"A few more minutes like this and we'll end up sleeping here tonight."

"That doesn't matter, either."

With a laugh, he turned his face to kiss her neck where the skin was still heated from excitement. Reluctantly he shifted his weight. "You know, with a few minor changes, we could be a great deal more comfortable."

"In the bed," she murmured in agreement, but merely snuggled into him.

"For a start. I'm thinking more of the long term."

It was difficult to think at all when he was warm and firm against her. "Which long term?"

"Both of us tend to do a lot of running around and overnight packing in order to spend the evening together."

"Mmmm. I don't mind."

He did. The more content he became with her, the more discontent he became with their arrangement. *I love you.* The words seemed so simple. But he'd never spoken them to a woman before. If he said them to her, how quickly would she pull away and disappear from his life? Some risks he wasn't ready to take. Cautious, he approached in the practical manner he thought she'd understand.

"Still, I think we could come up with a more logical arrangement."

She opened her eyes and shifted a bit. He could see there was already a line between her brows. "What sort of arrangement?"

He wasn't approaching this exactly as he'd planned. But then he'd learned that his usual meticulous plotting didn't work when he was dealing with A.J. "Your apartment's convenient to the city, where we both happen to be working at the moment."

"Yes." Her eyes had lost that dreamy softness they always had after loving. He wasn't certain whether to curse himself or her.

"We only work five days a week. My house, on the other hand, is convenient for getting away and relaxing. It seems a logical arrangement might be for us to live here during the week and spend weekends at my place.''

She was silent for five seconds, then ten, while dozens of thoughts and twice as many warnings rushed through her mind. ''A logical arrangement,'' he called it. Not a commitment, an ''arrangement.'' Or more accurately, an amendment to the arrangement they'd already agreed on. ''You want to live together.''

He'd expected more from her, anything more. A flicker of pleasure, a gleam of emotion. But her voice was cool and cautious. ''We're essentially doing that now, aren't we?''

''No.'' She wanted to distance herself, but his body kept hers trapped. ''We're sleeping together.''

And that was all she wanted. His hands itched to shake her, to shake her until she looked, really looked, at him and saw what he felt and what he needed. Instead he sat up and, in the unself-conscious way she always admired, began to dress. Feeling naked and defenseless, she reached for her blouse.

''You're angry.''

''Let's just say I didn't think we'd have to go to the negotiating table with this.''

''David, you haven't even given me five minutes to think it through.''

He turned to her then, and the heat in his eyes had her bracing. ''If you need to,'' he said with perfect calm, ''maybe we should just drop it.''

''You're not being fair.''

''No, I'm not.'' He rose then, knowing he had to get out, get away from her, before he said too much. ''Maybe I'm tired of being fair with you.''

''Damn it, David.'' Half-dressed, she sprang up to face him. ''You casually suggest that we should combine our living arrangements, then blow up because I need a few minutes to sort it through. You're being ridiculous.''

"It's a habit I picked up when I starting seeing you." He should have left. He knew he should have already walked out the door. Because he hadn't, he grabbed her arms and pulled her closer. "I want more than sex and breakfast. I want more than a quick roll in the sheets when our schedules make it convenient."

Furious, she swung away from him. "You make me sound like a—"

"No. I make us both sound like it." He didn't reach for her again. He wouldn't crawl. "I make us both sound like precisely what we are. And I don't care for it."

She'd known it would end. She'd told herself she'd be prepared when it did. But she wanted to shout and scream. Clinging to what pride she had left, she stood straight. "I don't know what you want."

He stared at her until she nearly lost the battle with the tears that threatened. "No," he said quietly. "You don't. That's the biggest problem, isn't it?"

He left her because he wanted to beg. She let him go because she was ready to.

Chapter Twelve

Nervous as a cat, A.J. supervised as folding chairs were set in rows in her mother's garden. She counted them—again—before she walked over to fuss with the umbrella-covered tables set in the side yard. The caterers were busy in the kitchen; the florist and two assistants were putting the finishing touches on the arrangements. Pots of lilies and tubs of roses were placed strategically around the terrace so that their scents wafted and melded with the flowers of Clarissa's garden. It smelled like a fairy tale.

Everything was going perfectly. With her hands in her pockets, she stood in the mid-morning sunlight and wished for a crisis she could dig her teeth into.

Her mother was about to marry the man she loved, the weather was a blessing and all of A.J.'s preplanning was paying off. She couldn't remember ever being more miserable. She wanted to be home, in her own apartment, with the door locked and the curtains drawn, with her head buried under the covers. Hadn't it been David who'd once told her that self-pity wasn't attractive?

Well, David was out of her life now, A.J. reminded herself. And had been for nearly two weeks. That was for the best. Without having him around, confusing her emotions, she could get on with business. The agency was so busy she was seriously considering increasing her staff. Because of the increased work load, she was on the verge of canceling her own two-week vacation in Saint Croix. She was personally negotiating two multimillion-dollar contracts and one wrong move could send them toppling.

She wondered if he'd come.

A.J. cursed herself for even thinking of him. He'd walked out of her apartment and her life. He'd walked out when she'd kept herself in a state of turmoil, struggling to keep strictly to the terms of their agreement. He'd been angry and unreasonable. He hadn't bothered to call and she certainly wasn't going to call him.

Maybe she had once, she thought with a sigh. But he hadn't been home. It wasn't likely that David Brady was mooning and moping around. A. J. Fields was too independent, and certainly too busy, to do any moping herself.

But she'd dreamed of him. In the middle of the night she'd pull herself out of dreams because he was there. She knew, better than most, that dreams could hurt.

That part of her life was over, she told herself again. It had been only an...episode, she decided. Episodes didn't always end with flowers and sunlight and pretty words. She glanced over to see one of the hired help knock over a line of chairs. Grateful for the distraction, A.J. went over to help set things to rights.

When she went back into the house, the caterers were busily fussing over quiche and Clarissa was sitting contentedly in her robe, noting down the recipe.

"Momma, shouldn't you be getting ready?"

Clarissa glanced up with a vague smile and petted the cat that curled in her lap. "Oh, there's plenty of time, isn't there?"

"A woman never has enough to time to get ready on her wedding day."

"It's a beautiful day, isn't it? I know it's foolish to take it as a sign, but I'd like to."

"You can take anything you want as a sign." A.J. started to move to the stove for coffee, then changed her mind. On impulse, she opened the refrigerator and pulled out one of the bottles of champagne that were chilling. The caterers muttered together and she ignored them. It wasn't every day a daughter watched her mother marry. "Come on. I'll help you." A.J. swung through the dining room and scooped up two fluted glasses.

"I wonder if I should drink before. I shouldn't be fuzzy headed."

"You should absolutely be fuzzy headed," A.J. corrected. Walking into her mother's room, she plopped down on the bed as she had as a child. "We should both be fuzzy headed. It's better than being nervous."

Clarissa smiled beautifully. "I'm not nervous."

A.J. sent the cork cannoning to the ceiling. "Brides have to be nervous. I'm nervous and all I have to do is watch."

"Aurora." Clarissa took the glass she offered, then sat on the bed beside her. "You should stop worrying about me."

"I can't." A.J. leaned over to kiss one cheek, then the other. "I love you."

Clarissa took her hand and held it tightly. "You've always been a pleasure to me. Not once, not once in your entire life, have you brought me anything but happiness."

"That's all I want for you."

"I know. And it's all I want for you." She loosened her grip on A.J.'s hand but continued to hold it. "Talk to me."

A.J. didn't need specifics to understand her mother meant David. She set down her untouched champagne and started to rise. "We don't have time. You need to—"

"You've had an argument. You hurt."

With a long, hopeless sigh, A.J. sank back down on the bed. "I knew I would from the beginning. I had my eyes open."

"Did you?" With a shake of her head, Clarissa set her glass beside A.J.'s so she could take both her hands. "Why is it you have such a difficult time accepting affection from anyone but me? Am I responsible for that?"

"No. No, it's just the way things are. In any case, David and I... We simply had a very intense physical affair that burned itself out."

Clarissa thought of what she had seen, what she had felt, and nearly sighed. "But you're in love with him."

With anyone else, she could have denied. With anyone else, she could have lied and perhaps have been believed. "That's my problem, isn't it? And I'm dealing with it," she added quickly, before she was tempted into self-pity again. "Today of all days we shouldn't be talking about anything but lovely things."

"Today of all days I want to see my daughter happy. How do you think he feels about you?"

It never paid to forget how quietly stubborn Clarissa could be. "He was attracted. I think he was a little intrigued because I wasn't immediately compliant, and in business we stood toe to toe."

Clarissa hadn't forgotten how successfully evasive her daughter could be. "I asked you how you think he feels."

"I don't know." A.J. dragged a hand through her hair and rose. "He wants me—or wanted me. We match very well in bed. And then I'm not sure. He seemed to want more—to get inside my head."

"And you don't care for that."

"I don't like being examined."

Clarissa watched her daughter pace back and forth in her quick, nervous gait. So much emotion bottled up, she thought. Why couldn't she understand she'd only truly feel it when she let it go? "Are you so sure that's what he was doing?"

"I'm not sure of anything, but I know that David is a very logical sort of man. The kind who does meticulous research into any subject that interests him."

"Did you ever consider that it was you who interested him, not your psychic abilities?"

"I think he might have been interested in one and uneasy about the other." She wished, even now, that she could be sure. "In any case it's done now. We both understood commitment was out of the question."

"Why?"

"Because it wasn't what he—what we," she corrected herself quickly, "were looking for. We set the rules at the start."

"What did you argue about?"

"He suggested we live together."

"Oh." Clarissa paused a moment. She was old-fashioned enough to be anxious and wise enough to accept. "To some, a step like that is a form of commitment."

"No, it was more a matter of convenience." Was that what hurt? she wondered. She hadn't wanted to analyze it. "Anyway, I wanted to think it over and he got angry. Really angry."

"He's hurt." When A.J. glanced over, surprised protest on the tip of her tongue, Clarissa shook her head. "I know. You've managed to hurt each other deeply, with nothing more than pride."

That changed things. A.J. told herself it shouldn't, but found herself weakening. "I didn't want to hurt David. I only wanted—"

"To protect yourself," Clarissa finished. "Sometimes doing one can only lead to the other. When you love someone, really love them, you have to take some risks."

"You think I should go to him."

"I think you should do what's in your heart."

Her heart. Her heart was broken open. She wondered why everyone couldn't see what was in it. "It sounds so easy."

"And it's the most frightening thing in the world. We can test, analyze and research psychic phenomena. We can set up labs in some of the greatest universities and institutions in the world, but no one but a poet understands the terror of love."

"You've always been a poet, Momma." A.J. sat down beside her again, resting her head on her mother's shoulder. "Oh, God, what if he doesn't want me?"

"Then you'll hurt and you'll cry. After you do, you'll pick up the pieces of your life and go on. I have a strong daughter."

"And I have a wise and beautiful mother." A.J. leaned over to pick up both glasses of wine. After handing one to Clarissa, she raised hers in a toast. "What shall we drink to first?"

"Hope." Clarissa clinked glasses. "That's really all there is."

A.J. changed in the bedroom her mother always kept prepared for her. It hadn't mattered that she'd spent only a handful of nights in it over nearly ten years; Clarissa had labeled it hers, and hers it remained. Perhaps she would stay there tonight, after the wedding was over, the guests gone and the newlyweds off on their honeymoon. She might think better there, and tomorrow find the courage to listen to her mother's advice and follow her heart.

What if he didn't want her? What if he'd already forgotten her? A.J. faced the mirror but closed her eyes. There were too many "what ifs" to consider and only one thing she could be certain of. She loved him. If that meant taking risks, she didn't have a choice.

Straightening her shoulders, she opened her eyes and studied herself. The dress was romantic because her mother preferred it. She hadn't worn anything so blatantly feminine and flowing in years. Lace covered her bodice and caressed her throat, while the soft blue silk peeked out of the eyelets. The skirt swept to a bell at her ankles.

Not her usual style, A.J. thought again, but there was something appealing about the old-fashioned cut and the charm of lace. She picked up the nosegay of white roses that trailed with ribbon and felt foolishly like a bride herself. What would it be like to be preparing to bond yourself with another person, someone who loved and wanted you? There would be flutters in your stomach. She felt them in her own.

Your throat would be dry. She lifted a hand to it. You would
feel giddy with a combination of excitement and anxiety.
She put her hand on the dresser to steady herself.

A premonition? Shaking it off, she stepped back from the
mirror. It was her mother who would soon promise to love,
honor and cherish. She glanced at her watch, then caught
her breath. How had she managed to lose so much time? If
she didn't put herself in gear, the guests would be arriving
with no one to greet them.

Alex's children were the first to arrive. She'd only met
them once, the evening before at dinner, and they were still
a bit awkward and formal with one another. But when her
future sister offered to help, A.J. decided to take her at her
word. Within moments, cars began pulling up out front and
she needed all the help she could get.

"A.J." Alex found her in the garden, escorting guests to
chairs. "You look lovely."

He looked a little pale under his tan. The sign of nerves
had her softening toward him. "Wait until you see your
bride."

"I wish I could." He pulled at the knot in his tie. "I have
to admit I'd feel easier if she were here to hold on to. You
know, I talk to millions of people every night, but this . . ."
He glanced around the garden. "This is a whole different
ball game."

"I predict very high ratings." She brushed his cheek.
"Why don't you slip inside and have a little shot of bour-
bon?"

"I think I might." He gave her shoulder a squeeze. "I
think I just might."

A.J. watched him make his way to the back door before
she turned back to her duties. And there was David. He
stood at the edge of the garden, where the breeze just ruf-
fled the ends of his hair. She wondered, as her heart began
to thud, that she hadn't sensed him. She wondered, as the
pleasure poured through her, if she'd wished him there.

He didn't approach her. A.J.'s fingers tightened on the wrapped stems of her flowers. She knew she had to take the first step.

She was so lovely. He thought she looked like something that had stepped out of a dream. The breeze that tinted the air with the scents of the garden teased the lace at her throat. As she walked to him, he thought of every empty hour he'd spent away from her.

"I'm glad you came."

He'd told himself he wouldn't, then he'd been dressed and driving south. She'd pulled him there, through her thoughts or through his own emotions, it didn't matter. "You seem to have it all under control."

She had nothing under control. She wanted to reach out to him, to tell him, but he seemed so cool and distant. "Yes, we're nearly ready to start. As soon as I get the rest of these people seated, I can go in for Clarissa."

"I'll take care of them."

"You don't have to. I—"

"I told you I would."

His clipped response cut her off. A.J. swallowed her longings and nodded. "Thanks. If you'll excuse me, then." She walked away, into the house, into her own room, where she could compose before she faced her mother.

Damn it! He swung away, cursing her, cursing himself, cursing everything. Just seeing her again had made him want to crawl. He wasn't a man who could live on his knees. She'd looked so cool, so fresh and lovely, and for a moment, just a moment, he'd thought he'd seen the emotions he needed in her eyes. Then she'd smiled at him as though he were just another guest at her mother's wedding.

He wasn't going to go on this way. David forced himself to make polite comments and usher well-wishers to their seats. Today, before it was over, he and A. J. Fields were going to come to terms. His terms. He'd planned it that way, hadn't he? It was about time one of his plans concerning her worked.

The orchestra A.J. had hired after auditioning at least a half-dozen played quietly on a wooden platform on the lawn. A trellis of sweat peas stood a few feet in front of the chairs. Composed and clear-eyed, A.J. walked through the garden to take her place. She glanced at Alex and gave him one quick smile of encouragement. Then Clarissa, dressed in dusky rose silk, stepped out of the house.

She looks like a queen, A.J. thought as her heart swelled. The guests rose as she walked through, but she had eyes only for Alex. And he, A.J. noted, looked as though no one else in the world existed but Clarissa.

They joined hands, and they promised.

The ceremony was short and traditional. A.J. watched her mother pledge herself, and fought back a sense of loss that vied with happiness. The words were simple, and ultimately so complex. The vows were timeless, and somehow completely new.

With her vision misted, her throat aching, she took her mother in her arms. "Oh, be happy, Momma."

"I am. I will be." She drew away just a little. "So will you."

Before A.J. could speak, Clarissa turned away and was swept up in an embrace by her new stepchildren.

There were guests to feed and glasses to fill. A.J. found keeping busy helped put her emotions on hold. In a few hours she'd be alone. Then she'd let them come. Now she laughed, brushed cheeks, toasted and felt utterly numb.

"Clarissa." David had purposely waited until she'd had a chance to breathe before he approached her. "You're beautiful."

"Thank you, David. I'm so glad you're here. She needs you."

He stiffened and only inclined his head. "Does she?"

With a sigh, Clarissa took both of his hands. When he felt the intensity, he nearly drew away. "Plans aren't necessary," she said quietly. "Feelings are."

David forced himself to relax. "You don't play fair."

"She's my daughter. In more ways than one."

"I understand that."

It took her only a moment, then she smiled. "Yes, you do. You might let her know. Aurora's an expert at blocking feelings, but she deals well with words. Talk to her?"

"Oh, I intend to."

"Good." Satisfied, Clarissa patted his hand. "Now I think you should try the quiche. I wheedled the recipe out of the caterer. It's fascinating."

"So are you." David leaned down to kiss her cheek.

A.J. all but exhausted herself. She moved from group to group, sipping champagne and barely tasting anything from the impressive display of food. The cake with its iced swans and hearts was cut and devoured. Wine flowed and music played. Couples danced on the lawn.

"I thought you'd like to know I read Steiger's script." After stepping beside her, David kept his eyes on the dancers. "It's extraordinary."

Business, she thought. It was best to keep their conversation on business. "Are you considering producing it?"

"Considering. That's a long way from doing it. I have a meeting with Steiger Monday."

"That's wonderful." She couldn't stop the surge of pleasure for him. She couldn't help showing it. "You'll be sensational."

"And if the script ever makes it to the screen, you'll have been the catalyst."

"I like to think so."

"I haven't waltzed since I was thirteen." David slipped a hand to her elbow and felt the jolt. "My mother made me dance with my cousin, and at the time I felt girls were a

lower form of life. I've changed my mind since." His ar
slid around her waist. "You're tense."

She concentrated on the count, on matching her steps
his, on anything but the feel of having him hold her agai
"I want everything to be perfect for her."

"I don't think you need to worry about that anymore.'

Her mother danced with Alex as though they were alo
in the garden. "No." She sighed before she could prevent i
"I don't."

"You're allowed to feel a little sad." Her scent was the.
as he remembered, quietly tempting.

"No, it's selfish."

"It's normal," he corrected. "You're too hard on you
self."

"I feel as though I've lost her." She was going to cry. A.
steeled herself against it.

"You haven't." He brushed his lips along her temple
"And the feeling will pass."

When he was kind, she was lost. When he was gentle, sh
was defenseless. "David." Her fingers tightened on h
shoulder. "I missed you."

It cost her to say it. The first layer of pride that covere
all the rest dissolved with the words. She felt his hand tens
then gentle on her waist.

"Aurora."

"Please, don't say anything now." The control she de
pended on wouldn't protect her now. "I just wanted you t
know."

"We need to talk."

Even as she started to agree, the announcement blare
over the mike. "All unmarried ladies, line up now for th
bouquet toss."

"Come on, A.J." Her new stepsister, laughing and ea
ger, grabbed her arm and hustled her along. "We have to se
who's going to be next."

She wasn't interested in bouquets or giddy young women. Her life was on the line. Distracted, A.J. glanced around for David. She looked back in time to throw up her hands defensively before her mother's bouquet landed in her face. Embarrassed, A.J. accepted the congratulations and well-meaning teasing.

"Another sign?" Clarissa commented as she pecked her daughter's cheek.

"A sign that my mother has eyes in the back of her head and excellent aim." A.J. indulged herself with burying her face in the bouquet. It was sweet, and promising. "You should keep this."

"Oh, no. That would be bad luck and I don't intend to have any."

"I'm going to miss you, Momma."

She understood—she always had—but she smiled and gave A.J. another kiss. "I'll be back in two weeks."

She barely had time for another fierce embrace before her mother and Alex dashed off in a hail of rice and cheers.

Some guests left, others lingered. When the first streaks of sunset deepened the sky she watched the orchestra pack up their instruments.

"Long day."

She turned to David and reached out a hand before she could help it. "I thought you'd gone."

"Just got out of the way for a while. You did a good job."

"I can't believe it's done." She looked over as the last of the chairs were folded and carted away.

"I could use some coffee."

She smiled, trying to convince herself to be light. "Do we have any left?"

"I put some on before I came back out." He walked with her to the house. "Where were they going on their honeymoon?"

The house was so empty. Strange, she'd never noticed just how completely Clarissa had filled it. "Sailing." She laughed a little, then found herself looking helplessly around the kitchen. "I have a hard time picturing Clarissa hoisting sails."

"Here." He pulled a handkerchief out of his pocket. "Sit down and have a good cry. You're entitled."

"I'm happy for her." But the tears began to fall. "Alex is a wonderful man and I know he loves her."

"But she doesn't need you to take care of her anymore." He handed her a mug of coffee. "Drink."

Nodding, she sipped. "She's always needed me."

"She still does." He took the handkerchief and dried her cheeks himself. "Just in a different way."

"I feel like a fool."

"The trouble with you is you can't accept that you're supposed to feel like a fool now and again."

She blew her nose, unladylike and indignant. "I don't like it."

"Not supposed to. Have you finished crying?"

She sulked a moment, sniffled, then sipped more coffee. "Yes."

"Tell me again that you missed me."

"It was a moment of weakness," she murmured into the mug, but he took it away from her.

"No more evasions, Aurora. You're going to tell me what you want, what you feel."

"I want you back." She swallowed and wished he would say something instead of just staring at her.

"Go on."

"David, you're making this difficult."

"Yeah, I know." He didn't touch her, not yet. He needed more than that. "For both of us."

"All right." She steadied herself with a deep breath. "When you suggested we live together, I wasn't expecting it. I wanted to think it through, but you got angry. Well, since you've been away, I've had a chance to think it through. I don't see why we can't live together under those terms."

Always negotiating, he thought as he rubbed a hand over his chin. She still wasn't going to take that last step. "I've had a chance to think it through, too. And I've changed my mind."

He could have slapped her and not have knocked the wind from her so successfully. Rejection, when it came, was always painful, but it had never been like this. "I see." She turned away to pick up her coffee, but her hands weren't nearly steady enough.

"You did a great job on this wedding, A.J."

Closing her eyes, she wondered why she felt like laughing. "Thanks. Thanks a lot."

"Seems to me like you could plan another standing on your head."

"Oh, sure." She pressed her fingers to her eyes. "I might go into the business."

"No, I was thinking about just one more. Ours."

The tears weren't going to fall. She wouldn't let them. It helped to concentrate on that. "Our what?"

"Wedding. Aren't you paying attention?"

She turned slowly to see him watching her with what appeared to be mild amusement. "What are you talking about?"

"I noticed you caught the bouquet. I'm superstitious."

"This isn't funny." Before she could stalk from the room he had caught her close.

"Damn right it's not. It's not funny that I've spent eleven days and twelve nights thinking of little but you. It's not funny that every time I took a step closer, you took one back. Every time I'd plan something out, the whole thing would be blown to hell after five minutes with you."

"It's not going to solve anything to shout at me."

"It's not going to solve anything until you start listening and stop anticipating. Look, I didn't want this any more than you did. I liked my life just the way it was."

"That's fine, then. I liked my life, too."

"Then we both have a problem because nothing's going to be quite the same again."

Why couldn't she breathe? Temper never made her breathless. "Why not?"

"Guess." He kissed her then, hard, angry, as if he wanted to kick out at both of them. But it only took an instant, a heartbeat. His lips softened, his hold gentled and she was molded to him. "Why don't you read my mind? Just this once, Aurora, open yourself up."

She started to shake her head, but his mouth was on hers again. The house was quiet. Outside, the birds serenaded the lowering sun. The light was dimming and there was nothing but that one room and that one moment. Feelings poured into her, feelings that once would have brought fear. Now they offered, requested and gave her everything she'd been afraid to hope for.

"David." Her arms tightened around him. "I need you to tell me. I couldn't bear to be wrong."

Hadn't he needed words? Hadn't he tried time and again to pry them out of her? Maybe it was time to give them to her. "The first time I met your mother, she said something to me about needing to understand or discover my own tenderness. That first weekend you stayed with me, I came home and found you sleeping on the bed. I looked at you, the woman who'd been my lover, and fell in love. The problem was I didn't know how to make you fall in love with me."

"I already had. I didn't think you—"

"The problem was you did think. Too much." He drew her away, only to look at her. "So did I. Be civilized. Be careful. Wasn't that the way we arranged things?"

"It seemed like the right way." She swallowed and moved closer. "It didn't work for me. When I fell in love with you, all I could think was that I'd ruin everything by wanting too much."

"And I thought if I asked, you'd be gone before the words were out." He brushed his lips over her brow. "We wasted time thinking when we should have been feeling."

She should be cautious, but there was such ease, such quiet satisfaction, in just holding him. "I was afraid you'd never be able to accept what I am."

"So was I." He kissed one cheek, then the other. "We were both wrong."

"I need you to be sure. I need to know that it doesn't matter."

"Aurora. I love you, who you are, what you are, how you are. I don't know how else to tell you."

She closed her eyes. Clarissa and she had been right to drink to hope. That was all there was. "You just found the best way."

"There's more." He held her, waiting until she looked at him again. And he saw, as he'd needed to, her heart in her eyes. "I want to spend my life with you. Have children with you. There's never been another woman who's made me want those things."

She took his face in her hands and lifted her mouth to his. "I'm going to see to it there's never another."

"Tell me how you feel."

"I love you."

He held her close, content. "Tell me what you want."

"A lifetime. Two if we can manage it."

* * * * *